The Indy Man

The Indy Man

Janet Dailey

OPEN ROAD
INTEGRATED MEDIA
NEW YORK

ISBN 978-1-4976-3958-4

This edition published in 2014 by Open Road Integrated Media, Inc.
345 Hudson Street
New York, NY 10014
www.openroadmedia.com

The Indy Man

Introduction

I ntroducing Janet Dailey's AMERICANA. Every novel in this collection is your passport to a romantic tour of the United States through time-honored favorites by America's First Lady of romance fiction. Each of the fifty novels is set in a different state, researched by Janet and her husband, Bill. For the Daileys it was an odyssey of discovery. For you, it's the journey of a lifetime.

Preface

When I first started writing back in the Seventies, my husband Bill and I were retired and traveling all over the States with our home—a 34' travel trailer—in tow. That's when Bill came up with the great idea of my writing a romance novel set in each one of our fifty states. It was an idea I ultimately accomplished before switching to mainstream fiction and hitting all the international bestseller lists.

As we were preparing to reissue these early titles, I initially planned to update them all—modernize them, so to speak, and bring them into the new high-tech age. Then I realized I couldn't do that successfully any more than I could take a dress from the Seventies and redesign it into one that would look as if it were made yesterday. That's when I saw that the true charm of these novels is their look back on another time and another age. Over the years, they have become historical novels, however recent the history. When you read them yourself, I know you will feel the same.

So, enjoy, and happy reading to all!

1

The candle flame flickered briefly despite the colored pear-shaped glass that rose protectively around it to keep away the drafts. It was a touch of intimate atmosphere in an otherwise well-lit lounge.

As Susan sipped the drink from her stemmed glass, the wavering light caught and reflected a red fire in the sleek curls of her dark brown hair. Salt rimmed the edges of her glass with crystal white thickness, some of it clinging to her lips when she replaced the glass on the small table. Unconsciously her tongue moistly cleansed the lower lip of its salt traces.

Her soft brown gaze swung to the man sitting opposite her. For the thousandth time Susan studied his aloof, almost arrogant features, the firm jaw, the thin hard mouth, the aristocraticaslly straight nose, the impassive dark, nearly black, eyes beneath thick brows of an equal shade. His hair was as dark as hers, but in this light it had a raven black sheen without the red casts hers possessed.

Warren Sullivan was not looking at Susan, though. His dark gaze was shifting about the lounge in that ever alert manner of his. He seemed suddenly withdrawn and remote, not actually with her but apart.

Leaning forward, Susan reached out with her hand to touch the long masculine fingers that held his glass. The movement caused the ruffled vee of

1

her white blouse to open, revealing a tantalizing glimpse of her lacy bra. The nearness of her hand to the candle flame illuminated the gold ring with its diamond fire. Her fingernails were impractically long and manicured, the way Warren liked them.

The touch of her hand against his brought the dark gaze to center on her face, cameo-smooth in tenderness. A semblance of a smile curved his mouth as Warren released the glass to let his fingers close over the tips of hers. Susan ignored the lack of warmth in his smile because she saw the look of approval in his eyes.

'We're going to have a good marriage, Susan.' The matter-of-fact announcement was issued quietly as if he had been pondering the question and was now satisfied with his conclusion.

Susan smiled, letting her dark lashes flutter down. She had become accustomed to Warren's statements. They were rarely romantic, but she didn't mind. He had never proposed to her, merely told her they were getting married. Her acceptance of his decision was taken for granted.

'May I ask the learned attorney what prompted him to reach such a verdict when the jury is still out?' she murmured, her lashes sweeping up so she could gaze at him with undisguised tenderness.

His mouth moved again into that thin line that was never quite a smile. 'Because, my dear, during the day you are level-headed and efficient. There's only the slightest trace of the womanly, feminine creature that you are at this moment. That is why we will have a good marriage: you are like me in that you don't want private emotions entangled with business.'

'Or business entangled with private emotions.'

'That too, of course.' His broad shoulders moved in an agreeing shrug as if that was of secondary importance. Susan held back a sigh.

There were times when she wondered if Warren really loved her. Fortunately there were times when he convinced her of it very thoroughly. She silently wished they were not here in this public place so that he would take her in his arms and convince her again.

Her fingertip trailed around the salted edge of her glass. Glancing up, she saw his gaze wandering about the room again. Almost as if he felt her watching him, he met the soft adoration of her look.

'I often wonder,' he mused, 'how long it might have been before I noticed you if my father hadn't become ill and I was not forced to stand in for him at the Christmas party. You had worked there for—how long—two years?'

'Four years,' Susan corrected gently. 'Two years in the typing pool and two years as your secretary.'

'I always thought you were very attractive,' Warren continued, not the least bit perturbed that he had not known how long she had been employed.

2

'But you were always so cool and practical that I never guessed such a warm, vibrant woman lived beneath that cloak of efficiency, not until you shed it that day at the party.'

'You have no idea, darling,' Susan murmured huskily, 'the cheer that went up that day when the female staff members of Sullivan, Sullivan and Holmes learned that you were going to attend the Christmas party.'

'Including from you?'

'My cheer was perhaps the loudest of all,' she smiled deeply. 'I told you I've been infatuated with you since almost the first day I saw you. But with all the socialites that paraded through your life, I never thought I had a chance.'

'Those empty-headed pieces of fluff,' he laughed in derision. 'I was never interested in any of them. I was looking for someone like you, intelligent and understanding, capable of appreciating the demands of my career and supporting my ambitions. Until I came to know you, I thought all women threw tantrums or became piqued if business interfered with the time I spent with them.'

'You should have dated a doctor's daughter before,' Susan laughed. 'I don't remember taking part in any school function that my father was able to see through to the end. Invariably some woman decided to have her baby in the middle of the performance. Not that I wasn't hurt sometimes, but my mother taught me patience and understanding. She had had plenty of time to learn.'

Susan knew Warren was listening to her, yet his head was half-turned to glance around the lounge. They were not expecting to meet anyone tonight and she wondered fleetingly why he was so interested in the other occupants. The budding curiosity didn't last longer than it took his look to return to her.

'I'm glad you're understanding,' he stated. Was it her imagination, or was his expression sterner than before? 'It's going to be a trying time at the office next week with my father going into hospital for surgery.'

'I'm certain the doctors will find that the tumor is benign,' Susan offered, realizing Warren's harshness had probably been a show of concern for his father's health. They were very close.

'Of course it will be,' he nodded curtly, sliding a glance again to the side, his mouth tightening grimly. 'Though naturally they'll have to run a biopsy on it to be certain.'

'Warren,' Susan tilted her head to the side, a tiny frown drawing her brows together, 'what's wrong?'

Impatience laced his expression. 'The man at the second table— No, don't look now,' he reprimanded in a low sharp voice. 'He's been rudely staring at you for the last ten minutes.'

'At me?' she repeated in disbelief. 'Are you certain?'

3

'Very,' Warren retorted.

'Maybe I know him. Maybe he's someone I went to school with,' Susan suggested hesitantly. 'The second table, did you say?'

'Yes. Take a look, but for heaven's sake don't be obvious about it,' he commanded.

An order that was much easier given than carried out. With forced nonchalance, Susan leaned back in her chair. She let her gaze wander idly about the lounge until it was caught by the man at the second table and held by his intent regard. There wasn't any doubt in Susan's mind that he was looking at no one else but her.

The man was alone at the table, leaning somewhat indolently back in his chair. A thumb was hooked in the waistband of his suit trousers, holding the jacket open to reveal a vest in the same unusual tobacco brown color as his suit. Even at this distance Susan could recognize the expensive tailoring.

His hair was a tawny shade, brown unusually gilded with dark gold, a trifle long judged by the clean-cut standards Warren adhered to, and its careless style gave the man a look suggesting the untamed. The lean, handsome face held deeply grooved lines around his mouth and eyes that said he smiled often. Boyish was an initial adjective that Susan wanted to use to describe the man, but he was much too virile and too masculine. That faintly boyish charm she detected was really the rakish air of a rogue. The stunningly handsome face and devastating smile had probably overwhelmed many women.

Her inspection finally stopped at his eyes, blue and glinting with undisguised amusement. Susan couldn't shake the feeling that there was something about him that was vaguely familiar. She stared at him a minute more while she tried to place what it was.

The stranger used that minute to inspect her insolently. As his blue eyes ran over her figure, Susan felt her clothes being stripped away little by little. The caressive quality of the sensation sent flames shooting through her veins but without any feeling of revulsion. She glanced away before she could ascertain why she had thought she might know him.

'Well?' Warren demanded impatiently.

A black anger was in his expression and Susan knew he had recognized the stranger's intimate appraisal of her at the last. Perhaps the only major fault that Warren possessed was his foul, brooding temper. She almost wanted to say that she knew the man, but at this point she didn't think Warren cared whether she did or not.

'I don't think I know him, although I have the feeling I've seen him somewhere before,' she replied evenly. It wouldn't do to let Warren see she had been embarrassed.

Warren flashed another glance at the man, his jaw tightening ominously as he let his gaze slide back to her. 'I can't believe the insolence of that man!'

'Just ignore him,' Susan shrugged.

'How can you ignore such a blatant disregard of good manners?' he snapped. 'It's about time someone taught him some.'

'Then you would be behaving as boorishly as he is,' she pointed out. Logic was the only way to penetrate Warren's temper. 'Besides,' she glanced out of the corner of her eye and saw the movement of the man rising to his feet, 'he's leaving anyway.'

Warren wasn't satisfied with Susan's word that the man was leaving and had to look for himself. His eyes were dark as pitch as they swung back to narrow on her face.

'Are you quite certain you don't know that man?' he demanded.

'I——-.' Susan hesitated, then invisibly shrugged away that vague sensation of something familiar about him. 'I'm quite certain,' she concluded with a firm nod of her head.

'Then would you tell me why,' Warren continued in the same ominously low tone, 'he's walking to our table?'

Her brown eyes widened in surprise. A hand moved bewilderedly to a wing of dark hair at her temple, smoothing it back to glance surreptitiously at the man. He was approaching their table with a rolling, supple walk totally unlike Warren's firm, almost military stride.

There was the faintest suggestion of a smile on the man's mouth, but his eyes were decidedly crinkled at the corners, a wicked glitter in their blueness. She had barely met his mocking look and she was glancing swiftly away.

Her mind raced. She didn't know him, did she? How could anyone forget someone like that? She didn't know him, she was sure of it. Yet why was he coming to their table? Warren never forgot a face or a name, so it couldn't be him the stranger was coming to see.

When the man stopped beside the table, Susan wasn't able to raise her head in inquiry. Her hands were trembling and she clasped them together, silently praying that Warren wouldn't notice how unnerved she was, and that he wouldn't make a scene.

'Excuse me,' the man spoke in a voice that was low and musically pitched.

Unwillingly Susan lifted her chin, determined to show the man how completely indifferent she was to his presence. But the laughing blue eyes weren't looking at her. The man's falsely solemn expression was directed at Warren, whose head tilted challengingly toward the man.

'You don't know me,' the man continued, erasing at least one of Susan's doubts. 'My name is Mitch Braden.' A bell rang in her mind, but not loudly enough for her to know why. A hand was extended toward Warren in greeting. 'I came over to offer an apology for my rudeness. I'm afraid I might have offended you by staring at your date.'

For only a brief second did the man's gaze swing to Susan before it centered again on Warren. The hand remained outstretched. In the face of Mitch Braden's apology, Warren grudgingly shook the man's hand, not mollified by the apology but unable to disregard it without displaying bad manners himself.

'Your apology is accepted,' Warren responded curtly, releasing the man's hand almost abruptly.

'Thank you, Mr.—I'm sorry, what was your name?' A smile flashed across Mitch Braden's face, deepening the grooves around his mouth and proving as devastatingly attractive as Susan had thought it would be.

'Sullivan, Warren Sullivan,' was the reluctant reply.

At that moment Warren had released the man's gaze so he missed the sudden twinkle that sparkled in the man's eyes, but Susan saw it. As if feeling her gaze, the man named Mitch Braden looked at her.

'I don't suppose you need me to tell you what a very beautiful woman your date is, Mr. Sullivan. Obviously you've had more opportunity to appreciate her looks than the few moments I have spent admiring her. It isn't often that a face as beautiful as hers has a figure to go with it.'

Susan breathed in sharply, unable to believe the man could speak so audaciously. Warren seemed momentarily stunned by the man's boldness as well.

'Mr. Braden,' he said cuttingly, 'I don't like your comments.'

An eyebrow of golden brown, the same color as the man's hair, raised in surprise. 'Don't you think she has a beautiful shape? I would say she's almost perfectly proportioned. Maybe you haven't taken a good look at her recently——.'

'Susan is very beautiful,' Warren interrupted angrily, black fire flashing from his eyes. 'But I certainly don't appreciate you saying things like that——.'

'I see,' Mitch Braden interrupted calmly. His laughing gaze swung to Susan's face, taking note of her heightened color. When he was looking at her, the man didn't attempt to conceal his mockery with pseudoinnocence. 'You're afraid too many compliments will go to her head, isn't that it? That's a pity, because she has such a pretty little head.' He glanced back at Warren's smoldering expression. 'Susan, did you say her name was Susan?'

'It happens to be Mrs. Sullivan. She's my wife!' Warren snapped.

Partially angered by the man's flirtatious remarks deliberately intended to rile Warren, Susan had still found herself hiding a smile. The tiny dimple in one cheek vanished at Warren's announcement.

'Congratulations,' Mitch Braden responded easily to the news, not displaying disappointment or surprise. 'You're a very lucky man, Mr. Sullivan.'

'Thank you,' Warren returned acidly.

When Mitch Braden glanced again at Susan, his vocal blue eyes said it was such a pity she was married, but his smiling voice spoke of something else.

'May I buy you two a drink and we can toast the happy couple?' he offered with a flashing smile.

Susan's heart accelerated slightly. 'No, thank you, Mr. Braden,' she refused in a swift, husky voice.

'We were just going into the dining room to eat,' Warren inserted to rescue her. 'Thank you just the same.'

The man inclined his head in shrugging acceptance. 'It was the least I could do to make up for my earlier bad manners.'

Warren rose to his feet. Susan was faintly surprised to see that Warren was an inch or so taller than Mitch Braden. The man's presence had so completely dominated the table that she had presumed him the taller of the two. Even now Mitch Braden was the more compelling.

'Your apology has been accepted, Mr. Braden,' Warren said coolly, touching Susan's shoulder to prompt her to her feet. 'Now please excuse us!'

'Of course.' The stunning smile seemed permanently carved on the handsome face, the sparkling blue eyes directed at each of them in turn. 'I hope you two have a long and happy marriage. If not,' the wicked glint returned as his gaze rested momentarily on Susan, 'I hope I'm around to pick up the pieces.'

Susan slipped her hand under Warren's elbow. 'We shall have a long and happy marriage, Mr. Braden. Good evening.'

With a curt nod in the general direction of Mitch Braden, Warren turned Susan toward the door. The muscles in his arms were rigidly hard as his striding walk practically carried her out of the lounge. She guessed at the taut hold he had on his temper. There was no need for her to turn around because she could feel Mitch Braden's eyes watch them leave.

Free of the room and Braden, Warren's rein on his temper relaxed. 'That man is insufferable!' he muttered beneath his breath. 'He apologizes, then tries to steal you from under my nose. It didn't even faze him when I told him you were my wife!'

'That was going to a bit of an extreme, wasn't it?' she suggested gently. 'I mean, we aren't married yet.'

'Simply because it isn't convenient right now,' Warren snapped. 'And August is only a little over two months away and we're getting married then.'

'Yes,' Susan agreed, but Warren's white lie bothered her.

Warren continued as if he hadn't heard her. 'Do you know this is the first time I've wanted to invite a man to go outside with me since I was in high school and beat up the local bully?'

The story had been told to her several times before, so she merely nodded and was secretly relieved that Warren had not embarrassed her tonight by trying to repeat a high school episode. Warren, embarrassing her? The idea was so ludicrous considering how proper and polite Warren was that she nearly laughed aloud.

'Let's forget about that man,' she suggested instead, and wondered why she didn't believe her own words.

'You're right, of course.' The taut lines of anger vanished as Warren looked down his nose at her.

'There isn't any need to let his impudence spoil our evening. Shall we dine here as planned? I don't think that man will bother us again.'

Susan wasn't as certain about that as Warren seemed to be, but she agreed with his suggestion anyway. Besides, she told herself as the dining room hostess led them to a table, she should look on the bright side of the otherwise unfortunate episode. At least she had learned that Warren was capable of being jealous. Sometimes he was so self-contained that she wondered if she aroused any feelings in him at all.

They were studying the menu when a group of loud, laughing voices invaded the dining room. Susan's back was to the entrance but she didn't need to turn around to learn who had entered.

'Good lord!' Warren exclaimed irritably. 'It's that man Braden again with a motley collection of men! The hostess is leading them this way. Pretend not to notice them, Susan.'

How could anyone fail to notice the boisterous group coming nearer? Susan tried to obey Warren's crisp command by concentrating on the menu, but as the men filed past their table, she couldn't resist peering above the leather-bound menu.

There were six men in the group, counting Mitch Braden. If he had noticed Susan and Warren, there was no indication of it now. He was laughing at some comment that had come from the gangly youth bringing up the rear.

It was an odd assortment, average men running from short to tall, skinny to thin, young to old. None of them possessed the strikingly handsome looks of the man leading the way.

The large table the hostess led them to was not far from Susan and Warren. Susan breathed a silent sigh of relief when Mitch Braden took a chair that faced away from them. She doubted if she could have eaten with him watching her at his leisure. Warren, too, seemed to relax.

After receiving Susan's preference for her meal, Warren gave the waiter their order, spending a few minutes choosing a wine from the dining room's wine list. He prided himself on being a connoisseur with very discriminating taste. Susan had difficulty telling one wine from another.

When the main course was served, the waiter uncorked the chilled bottle and offered a tasting portion to Warren. 'Sir ——-' the waiter began.

8

'This is not the wine I ordered,' Warren interrupted immediately, not allowing the man a chance to finish. He reached for the bottle still in the waiter's hands. 'This wine was not even on your list.'

'No, sir,' the man agreed. 'It's from the owner's private stock. Compliments of the gentleman at the large table.'

Mitch Braden. Both Warren and Susan darted a look at him. He had turned in his chair and briefly inclined his head in acknowledgment.

'The owner?' Susan breathed, glancing curiously at the waiter.

'He is a friend of the owner, I believe,' was the courteous answer.

Indecision held Warren silent for an instant. Susan guessed that he wanted to refuse the wine. It must have been a very excellent vintage because he did not.

'Please thank the gentleman for us,' Warren said tautly.

'Of course, sir.'

Perhaps if Mitch Braden had not sent the wine to their table, Susan might have been better able to ignore his presence in the dining room. As it was, her eyes strayed often to his table, focusing on his lean masculine form and the dark golden-toast shade of his hair. Never once during the entire meal did she encounter the laughing blue eyes with the crinkled lines at the corners.

Always from the table of six there was laughter and constant chatter. In comparison the silence between Susan and Warren seemed unnatural. But Warren didn't care for any discussions during a meal. The time for talk was before or after, but never during a meal. By the time coffee was served, a tiny pain had begun to hammer at her temples, from tension, Susan guessed.

Laughter punctuated the air, coming naturally from Mitch Braden's table. Warren cast a censorious look in that direction.

'It would have been an excellent meal if the atmosphere had been more peaceful,' he commented.

Lifting her chin slightly, Susan refused to let her gaze wander to the other table. 'I imagine about the only place you can be fairly certain of obtaining a quiet meal is in your own home.'

'Very true,' Warren agreed, dry-voiced. 'Are we ready to leave?' At Susan's nod, he signaled their waiter for the bill.

When he rose and walked to the back of her chair, Susan noticed one of the men nudge Mitch Braden. She could barely see his lips move, but she knew instinctively that he was telling Mitch that she and Warren were leaving.

One shoulder lifted in an uncaring gesture and some comment was made in response by the man. A stout balding man laughed shortly and said, 'When did that ever stop you?' Mitch Braden's low answer brought laughter from the rest of the group.

Holding her breath for fear he might have heard the exchange too, Susan glanced swiftly at Warren. He merely looked inquiringly back and she smiled with false brightness.

From the restaurant, Warren drove her straight home with no stops in between. It was a week night, which meant they both had to be at the office in the morning. Warren did not believe in keeping late hours when he had to work the next day. For that matter, neither did Susan. On Tuesdays and Thursdays, the only week nights they went out, it was strictly for dinner, then home. The weekends were quite different.

This night Susan was glad to have the evening end quickly. It hadn't been as enjoyable as other outings. Mostly because of Mitch Braden.

Their goodnight embrace in the parked car outside her home did not last long. Lingering kisses were saved for the weekends when they had more time to indulge in them. At those times, Warren was masterful and passionate. Susan had never considered it odd that those were the times when she was most aware that she loved him.

Only when she was in the house and watching his car drive away did she wish for the first time that the pattern of their relationship hadn't become so predictable. A surprise now and then would be nice.

Of course, Mitch Braden, whoever he was, had provided a surprise this night and it hadn't been so nice. Oh, Warren had displayed jealousy, but Susan still wished the encounter had never occurred. Just why she wished that she didn't know.

'Is that you, Susan?' her mother called.

She turned away from the window. 'Yes, Mom, it's me,' she answered, shedding her spring coat and hanging it in the closet before walking down the hallway to the large family room.

'Hello, honey, did you have a nice time?' her father, Doctor Simon Mabry, greeted her as she entered the room. His burly frame was draped in a reclining chair, a medical magazine unopened on his lap.

'Of course,' Susan smiled.

'Is *he* here?' Her younger brother Greg, a week away from turning seventeen, twisted away from the television set to glance at her.

"No, Warren didn't come in tonight.' Susan picked up a pillow from the couch and threw it at her brother's lanky frame sprawled on the floor. Warren and Greg had disliked each other on first sight and the months since their first meeting hadn't changed either's opinion.

As Susan slipped off her shoes and started to curl her feet beneath her to sit on the couch, the pillow was thrown back. She caught it easily from long practice.

"Ouch, Mother! You're pulling my hair!' the youngest of the Mabrys exclaimed angrily—Amy, age thirteen.

10

'Well, if you would hold still———-' Beth Mabry began, Susan's mother.

'You'd pull out every hair in my head!' Amy squeaked, her hands moving protectively to her long auburn hair.

'I have to get the tangles out somehow, unless you'd rather do it yourself.' Beth Mabry firmly pulled the young girl closer to her chair. 'After all, you were the one who got it into this mess, climbing that tree like a tomboy.'

'I told you,' Amy protested with rounded brown eyes of speaking innocence, 'I had to get Peggy Fraser's kitten. Ouch!'

"Want me to comb it for you, Amy?' Susan offered, knowing the tug-of-war could go on continuously between mother and daughter.

As her mother had put it the night before when she and Amy had argued, Amy was 'going through that difficult stage,' crazy about boys and becoming a woman but not quite able to stop climbing trees.

'Oh, yes, please, Susan!' Amy agreed fervently.

'Will you guys pipe down?' Greg protested impatiently. 'I'm trying to watch this TV show!'

'Keep it to a low roar, Amy,' her father suggested with a gentle smile.

'Greg's much too bossy, Dad.' Amy stuck out her tongue at her brother as she walked to the couch where Susan sat.

Slowly and carefully working the snarls free from Amy's hair, Susan smiled to herself. It was no wonder that Warren found it difficult to relax when he came here. He had been an only child and the constant wrangling that went on between brother and sister and parent was something he couldn't accept. He would adjust to it when they started having children of their own.

The television program her father and brother were watching was a police drama. Susan managed to grasp most of the storyline without giving the picture her complete attention. The local Indianapolis news broadcast came on as she brushed the last snarl from Amy's long auburn hair. She listened to the news and the weather, but when the subject shifted to sports, Susan started to untangle her legs from beneath her and stand up.

A familiar face appeared on the television screen. She stared at it in disbelief. It was Mitch Braden, the man she had so disastrously met with Warren tonight. Only on television he wasn't wearing that perfectly tailored suit and vest. He wore a tee shirt that stretched like a second skin over his chest, and snug-fitting Levis. The film was taken outside and the wind was ruffling the dark tawny gold of his hair.

'Is … is that Mitch Braden?' Susan forced the question out, too stunned to hear what the sports announcer was saying.

'Yep,' Greg replied.

The smiling, handsome face left the screen and a rundown of baseball scores started.

'Who is he?' Susan asked hesitantly.

'He's Mitch Braden.' Greg frowned at the dumbness of her question.

'But—what does he do?'

'What does he *do*?' Greg exclaimed with a taunting hoot. 'He's just about the most famous race car driver around. He's in town for the Indianapolis 500 race Memorial weekend. What does he do! Boy, what a dumb sister!'

'I thought he looked familiar,' she commented, but more to herself than as a direct comment.

'Well, you just saw him on the television screen.' Greg shook his head in despair at her strange remark.

'No, I mean, tonight at the restaurant,' Susan explained absently, still slightly stunned that Mitch Braden had turned out to be such a famous personality.

'You saw him! You saw Mitch Braden!' Her brother bounded to his feet. 'Did you get his autograph? Did you talk to him?'

'Well, yes, I talked to him in a way, but I didn't recognize him. I knew he looked familiar, but I didn't know why.'

'You didn't get his autograph!' Greg moaned.

'What did he say to you?' Amy asked curiously. 'Is he as handsome as he looks on television?'

'Mostly he talked to Warren,' Susan answered truthfully, wishing suddenly that she hadn't even mentioned that she had seen him. 'He's good-looking.' More so than on camera, she thought silently, because film couldn't capture the magnetism he exuded.

'I wasn't aware that Warren was acquainted with anyone in racing circles,' her father included himself in the conversation.

Greg's hair, a dark brown like Susan's, fell shaggily across his forehead. He flipped it away from his eyes with his hand. 'Neither was I,' he agreed forcefully.

Susan bit into her lower lip. She wasn't about to explain what had really happened. 'Warren doesn't know him.'

'You said he talked to him,' Greg reminded.

'They were simply in the same restaurant at the same time.' Susan rose to her feet to bring an end to the conversation. 'It was just a case of two strangers exchanging casual conversation. I wouldn't even have mentioned it if I'd known I was going to get the third degree.'

She started for the hall with Greg trailing on her heels.

'I don't suppose Weighty Warren knew who Mitch Braden was either.'

'Will you stop making those insulting references about my fiancé?' Susan demanded impatiently. 'And no, he didn't know who he was any more than I did.'

'That figures,' Greg responded derisively.

'There are more important things in the world, Greg,' Susan stamped her bare foot on the floor, a childish action for someone approaching her twenty-fourth birthday, 'than knowing some idiot who drives around a racetrack at a hundred and fifty miles an hour.'

'Yeah?' her brother challenged.

'Greg!' came her mother's warning voice.

'Ah, gee, Mom,' he turned impatiently away from Susan. 'There's only a chance in a million of meeting someone like Mitch Braden and my sister blew it!'

Susan didn't wait to hear what arguments Beth Mabry offered in her behalf. She escaped to her room while she had the chance, knowing that she probably hadn't heard the last of her brother's recriminations or Mitch Braden's name.

2

'Susan, is my son busy?'

Glancing up from her typewriter, Susan encountered the solemn face of Robert Sullivan, the senior partner of the law firm and Warren's father. The resemblance between the two was striking. Both were tall and ruggedly handsome. Warren's hair was jet black while his father's had turned iron gray.

'Yes, he is,' she nodded. 'You can go on in, Mr. Sullivan.'

She gestured fleetingly toward the closed interoffice door behind her, wondering if she would ever be able to address the man less formally even after she and Warren were married.

Robert Sullivan always seemed so remote and untouchable, the way Warren did sometimes.

With a sigh, Susan turned backed to the typewriter, rereading the last page of the corporate agreement for typographical errors. Satisfied that there were no mistakes, she removed the original and carboned sheet from the carriage. The hall door opened as she started to staple the several-page document together.

'Hi.' Greg ambled into her office, hands stuffed in the pockets of his thin jacket.

'Hello.' Her surprise at his unexpected appearance was in her voice. 'What are you doing downtown?'

'I had to take care of my car insurance,' he answered with a shrug of his shoulders. 'I thought I'd stop by to see if you wanted a ride home.'

Susan glanced at her watch. It was only a few minutes before five o'clock, which was her normal leaving time.

'Warren was going to take me home, but———.' She looked to the closed interoffice door. With his father in there, there was no telling how long he would be tied up.

'Oh, that's okay. I just thought I'd check.' Greg started to turn back toward the hall door.

'Greg?' The atmosphere had been tense between Susan and her brother since she had lost her temper two nights before after his disparaging reference to Warren. She guessed his offer of a ride was a conciliatory gesture. He stopped and pivoted toward her. 'I'm not sure———' she began, only to come to a halt as the door to Warren's office opened.

'Susan———' Warren walked in, an absent frown clouding his wide forehead. At the sight of her brother, he paused and nodded. 'Hello, Gregory. I didn't expect to see you here.'

Susan felt her brother's wince. He disliked the use of his full name. No matter how tactfully she mentioned it to Warren, he still persisted in using it.

'I stopped to see if Susan needed a ride home,' her brother explained tautly. His chin was thrust defiantly forward and there was a belligerent darkness in the brown gaze that met Warren's.

'Well, that's opportune,' he smiled coldly, and Susan despaired of the two ever becoming friends. Warren's obsidian dark eyes looked toward her. 'I was just coming in to suggest that it might be better if you left without me. My father and I have some business to go over, cases I might need to handle while he's in the hospital. It might take considerable time.'

'I understand,' she smiled. 'I'll go home with Greg.' She hesitated, disliking to mention dinner that evening since he hadn't. 'What about dinner tonight?'

'I'll phone you at home. I'm not certain how long I'll be,' he answered, not expressing any regret in words or his tone of voice that their plans for the evening might be canceled.

'Of course.' Susan turned away, a barely audible sigh of disappointment escaping with the words she spoke.

'Since Gregory is already here and it's nearly five, you might as well leave whenever you've straightened up,' Warren stated in dismissal.

'I've finished the Hoxworth proposal,' she said, picking up the document she had just stapled together. 'Did you want it now or in the morning?'

'I'll take it now.' He reached for the papers in her hands, briefly leafing through them as he turned again toward his office.

'I understand you met Mitch Braden the other night,' Greg spoke up unexpectedly.

Warren stopped short and glanced piercingly over his shoulder at Susan, condemnation in his look.

'I forgot to mention to you, Warren,' Susan hastened to explain how Greg had known about their meeting with Mitch Braden, 'why he looked so familiar to me. Mitch Braden is a racing car driver. He's in town for the Indianapolis 500 race.'

'A racing car driver?' There was a faintly contemptuous curl to Warren's mouth. 'I suppose that explains his behavior.'

When the door to his office had closed behind Warren, Susan could feel Greg's eyes watching her. 'What did he mean by that?' he asked finally.

She didn't look up but continued clearing her desk in preparation to leave. 'Let's just say that your idol Mr. Braden behaved a little rudely the other night and leave it at that.'

'With a snob like your boyfriend, I wouldn't blame him,' her brother retorted.

Susan counted slowly to ten. 'You don't know what you're talking about, and Warren is not a snob,' she replied patiently. 'And I have no intention of arguing about it or discussing it any further. Okay?'

'Okay,' Greg submitted grudgingly.

A quarter of an hour later, Susan was gingerly sliding into the passenger seat of Greg's vintage Chevrolet, a tactful term for a worn-out used car. She carefully avoided the jutting edge of broken plastic ribbing on the seat that was trying to snag her pantyhose.

'I thought you were going to buy new covers for the seats,' she commented as she brushed her plaid skirt of olive green and black on white.

Her brother grinned and turned the key in the ignition. 'I'm hoping Mom and Dad will buy them as a birthday present. Then I can use the money I saved to buy some hubcaps.'

'You might be further ahead to save the money for a down payment on a new car,' Susan suggested when the motor grudgingly growled to life. 'It might prove a better investment.'

'This car is practically an antique. It's going to be worth a lot of money some day.'

'Yes, but will it be worth as much money as you invested in it? That's the question,' she teased, but with a thread of seriousness.

'She runs like a top,' Greg defended.

Her brother was practically a fanatic about the car. He and his friends spent hours tinkering with it after school and on weekends.

As they joined the rush hour traffic on the freeway en route to their home on the outskirts of Indianapolis, Susan admitted that outside of a grumbling reluctance to start the car ran quite well.

They were nearly halfway home when Greg murmured a worried 'Oh, oh!' and began to edge the car into the outside lane of traffic. Susan glanced curiously at his troubled frown.

'What's wrong?'

'The engine is overheating,' he answered, slowing the car to a stop on the wide shoulder of the freeway.

'Why?'

'That's what I'm about to find out,' Greg answered grimly as he opened his door and walked to the front of the car to raise the hood.

A misty gray cloud swirled into the air when the hood came up. Alarmed, Susan quickly opened her door and joined her cursing brother now standing several steps from the front of the car.

'Is it on fire?' she asked anxiously, not seeing any flames that might be causing the smoke.

'No, that's steam,' he sighed heavily. 'The radiator hose has a leak.'

'Can you fix it?' Susan followed Greg as he moved closer to inspect the problem when the bulk of the steam had dissipated. She was careful not to come too close to the front of the car in case the condensing steam stained her skirt or the well tailored blazer-style jacket of matching olive green.

'Even if I could fix it temporarily,' he grumbled, 'there isn't any place to get water to replace what the radiator has lost, which looks like about all of it.'

'Which means?' Susan prodded.

'Which means,' his hands were disgustedly propped on his hips as he looked past the car in the direction they had just come from, 'I'm going to have to hike to that service station a mile and a half back and see if they don't have a wrecker that can tow us in. And that means I'm going to have to spend the money I was saving for my hubcaps.'

'Greg' I'm sorry,' Susan offered sympathetically. 'I'll pay the towing charges as part of your birthday present. I———.'

'Hello, Susan. Are you having trouble?'

Whirling around, Susan's heart skipped a beat as she met the winning smile of Mitch Braden. His supple, rolling walk was carrying him from the cobalt blue sports car parked ahead of them.

There was an absent recognition that his twinkling eyes matched the color of his car or vice versa, but mostly Susan simply felt stunned amazement. The traffic had been so heavy that she had not noticed any cars even slowing in response to their breakdown, let alone hear any stop.

17

'How … How did you know it was me?' she breathed, still in a state of confused astonishment.

His gaze swept her from head to toe and back. 'I pride myself on never forgetting a figure,' he grinned wickedly, 'or a face.'

His suggestive reply disturbed her heartbeat, making it pulse much too fast. Susan turned away, momentarily unable to counter his remark.

Out of the corner of her eye, she caught a glimpse of her brother's slightly open-mouthed stare, as if he couldn't believe his eyes. For that matter neither could she. Who would ever have dreamed of Mitch Braden stopping to help?

A sickening thought knotted her stomach. What if he mentioned in front of Greg her supposed marriage to Warren? She would never be able to endure that man's mockery if he learned Warren had been lying.

'What's the problem?' Mitch Braden was directly behind her, his voice low and amused.

'Oh … er … a leak in the radiator hose.' Greg pulled himself out of his trance with a supreme effort.

Mitch Braden leaned forward to look under the hood and verify the problem. Susan moved quickly to the side of the car. The man was a wolf. She didn't intend there to be any 'accidental' physical contact between them—he would be too quick to find a way to take advantage of it.

Mitch Braden straightened, his expression serious as he darted her a twinkling look. 'It's a busted hose all right.'

'I'm Greg Mabry, Susan's brother,' Greg rushed, the shock at meeting the race driver wearing off. 'Boy, I can't believe I'm actually meeting you in person, Mr. Braden. I've watched you drive hundreds of times, on television mostly, but—wow, this is really a thrill for me!'

'I'm happy to meet you, too, Greg.' Mitch Braden offered his hand, which Greg shook with obvious enthusiasm.

'This was worth breaking down for,' her brother grinned, a quaking excitement trembling beneath the surface of his voice as if he was mentally pinching himself to be certain this was really happening to him.

'Greg, it's getting late,' Susan thinly prodded him back to the problem at hand.

'What?' He looked at her blankly for an instant. 'Oh, yeah.'

The grooves deepened around Mitch Braden's mouth as Susan's glance ricocheted away from his face. 'Why don't you let me give you a lift to the nearest wrecker service, Greg, and we'll make arrangements to have your car towed in?' he offered.

'Would you?' Greg breathed excitedly. 'I mean—wow, that would be terrific!'

18

Susan felt an overwhelming desire to give her brother a hard shake. His blatant hero-worship of the man was getting on her nerves. More than that, however, she wanted to bring this meeting to an end.

'Lock up your car and we'll go,' the man ordered easily.

'There's no need to do that,' Susan inserted quickly. 'I'll stay here and keep an eye on it until Greg comes back with the wrecker.'

'I can't let you do that.' Mitch Braden moved his head to the side in disagreement, a mocking glint in his blue eyes. 'A beautiful woman like you, stranded on a highway, that would be asking for trouble. I would never be able to face your husband if something happened to you while your brother and I were gone.'

Husband. There it was. And Greg picked up on it immediately as Susan's heart sunk to her toes.

'Husband?' he frowned. 'Susan isn't married.'

There was no mistaking the reason for the gleam in Mitch Braden's eyes as they swung to Greg. 'She isn't? This Warren——'

'That creep!' her brother grunted.

'Greg!' Susan warned through gritted teeth.

He paid no attention to her. 'She's engaged to him all right,' her brother acknowledged in the same contemptuous voice, 'but she isn't married to him yet.'

'It doesn't sound as if you're very much in favor of the marriage,' Mitch Braden observed.

'That's putting it mildly,' Greg replied, indifferent to his sister's daggers.

'Maybe you and I will have to join forces to see what we can do about it,' he suggested with a crooked smile.

'That's a good idea,' her brother laughed, suddenly seeing himself in the role of a matchmaker and liking the idea of Susan and Mitch Braden together.

'If you don't mind——' Anger trembled through her into her voice.

'You're right.' Mitch Braden nodded, his brown hair glinting golden as it caught the fire of the setting sun. 'This conversation isn't getting your car fixed.'

'Right,' Greg agreed. 'I'll lock up.'

He shut the hood and walked around to the driver's side to lock the doors. Susan wanted to dig her heels in and refuse to leave the car. Meeting Mitch's challenging look, she knew she couldn't leave Greg alone with him. There was no telling what kind of a scheme he would talk her gullible brother into trying.

Her brown eyes snapped with frustrated anger as she stalked past him toward the blue sports car. Of all the motorists on the highways, why had he been the one to stop? She paused beside the passenger door of the low-slung sports car and Mitch Braden was instantly beside her, his lazy, rolling stride covering ground with surprising swiftness.

19

'You'll have to wait for your brother,' he murmured in a mocking tone. 'It'll be easier for him to crawl into the back cubbyhole than for you with your skirt.'

She stared through the tinted glass window at the bucket seats in front of the half-seat behind them. What he said was irritatingly correct, and Susan wondered why he couldn't drive a car with full seats in front and back. Impatiently she glanced back to see her brother jogging toward them. His eyes widened in admiration as he approached the sports car.

'A Ferrari Boxer!' Greg whistled, touching the shiny blue surface almost reverently.

'She's a beauty, isn't she?' Mitch smiled understandingly as he opened the door.

'I'll say!' her brother agreed fervently, ducking his head inside to look around before crawling automatically into the compartment behind the bucket seats.

Susan's lips tightened grimly as she slid onto the leather seat, keeping her gaze straight ahead while Mitch closed the door. Greg leaned forward to inspect the dashboard panel and the gearshift on the floor between the front seats.

'I've only seen these babies in magazines,' he breathed in the same awed tone as before when Mitch slipped behind the wheel.

'This one has been all rebuilt to pass the emission control standards,' Mitch explained as the powerful motor sprang to life.

Susan refused to appear impressed, instead looking uninterestedly out of the window. The car accelerated quickly into the mainstream of traffic, the hand near her leg smoothly shifting the gears. She sat very still in prim silence.

'I saw you on television the other night,' Greg offered after they had traveled some distance.

'Did you?' Mitch responded absently as if it was a commonplace occurrence that didn't warrant any special mention.

'How do you think you'll do in the time trials for the Indy 500?'

'If the car keeps running the way it did today, it ought to finish somewhere up in the top ten,' he replied.

'The newspapers say you have the fastest car,' Greg observed.

'Maybe,' Mitch shrugged, 'but in a race as long as the Indy 500, there are too many unknowns that can happen for owning the fastest car to make you a sure winner.'

'Yeah,' her brother agreed with a smile. 'A lot depends on the driver behind the wheel and you're the best driver on the circuit.'

'With you and luck on my side,' Mitch grinned over his shoulder, 'I won't need a cheering section to win. Of course, there are some other guys in the race who are just as intent on making that victory lap as I am.'

20

'Oh sure,' Greg admitted, 'but you'll win. I know it.'

A low chuckle followed her brother's positive statement. Susan reluctantly acknowledged to herself that it was an attractive sound, warm and caressing like his voice. Her fingers tightened convulsively on the handle of her purse, not wanting to like anything about this man.

Out of the corner of her eye, she studied the strong hands gripping the wheel. Muscles rippled in the tan arms, bare below the short sleeves of his shirt. She considered the strength that the fingers, hands and arms had to possess to manhandle a car traveling at upward of a hundred and eighty miles or more.

Yet something told her they could be gentle, too. The prospect of them ever touching her with that gentleness was disturbing and she mentally shook the thought away.

They had made the turnaround on the highway and were driving into the station that had been Greg's destination when he had intended to walk for help. Cutting the motor, Mitch stepped from the car and Greg scrambled over the driver's seat to follow him.

Taking a step, Greg turned back, glancing into the car at Susan. 'You might as well wait here until I find out whether they can help me now.'

Susan had turned slightly, reaching for the door handle, but at her brother's words she subsided into the molding cushions of the leather seat. No doubt with Mitch Braden lending his voice to Greg's request, they would receive speedy service, she thought with a sigh.

The cynicism in the thought surprised her. What was there about the man that acted on her like two opposing fields of a magnet? She was unquestionably drawn by his charm and stunning looks. It was only natural that she found him physically attractive.

Yet something inside her insisted that she keep a safe distance from Mitch Braden. Susan wanted to believe it was a sense of fidelity to Warren, but that was only a part of it. There was a feeling of guilt, too, that she would be attracted to a man who was not her fiancé.

She brushed a wing of dark hair away from her cheek. Propping her elbow on the door, she rested her chin in her hand, trying to discern why she couldn't bring herself to trust Mitch Braden, and why she was so determined not to let herself like him.

The door on the driver's side was opened. Susan turned with a start as Mitch Braden slid behind the wheel and closed the door. The motor growled at the turn of the ignition key and he shifted the gear into reverse.

'Where's Greg? Susan looked frantically around.

Deftly they had turned around, the car fluidly changing from a reverse motion to forward with barely a break. The car was responsive to Mitch Braden's slightest touch, its power an extension of the man who commanded it.

Turning in her seat to look out the rear window, she saw Greg waving a casual goodbye.

'It will be ten minutes before a man is free to take the wrecker out for your brother's car,' Mitch finally explained when her frantic gaze riveted itself on his profile. 'Then they still have to install the new hose. I offered to give you a ride home.'

'Don't I have some say in it?' Susan protested with astonishment at his high-handed manner.

'I have your brother's permission.' He sent her a wicked smile. 'And I thought by the time you had finished all your objections about why you didn't want to ride with me, I would have you home.'

Susan breathed in deeply and finally expelled the breath in an impotently angry sigh.

'What's the matter?' he mocked. 'Don't you think I will take you straight home?'

'Will you?' she returned acidly.

'No side trips,' Mitch assured her with a mock promise, his blue eyes sparkling with an audacious light. 'Of course with such precious cargo, I'll take my time.'

'I think, Mr. Braden, that you're impossible,' she retorted tightly.

'Call me Mitch. And what warm-blooded male would deprive himself of such beautiful company sooner than he had to?' he grinned.

Susan turned her head away, a faint warmth creeping into her limbs. She had to remind herself how easily he issued compliments. She mustn't let them go to her head.

'Would you please not talk to me that way?' she requested icily, her fingers nervously clutching the purse in her lap.

'You don't like me to say that I think you're beautiful, is that it?' he rephrased the compliment with infuriating calm.

'That's it,' she tried to reply in the same vein.

'Okay,' Mitch agreed with a faint shrug.

They drove for a time in a silence that was unnerving for Susan. She simply couldn't seem to relax. Every muscle was taut with her inner tension.

'Do you know something, Susan?' he spoke finally in a thoughtful tone. 'You're the first woman who's kissed me today.'

'That must be a record,' was her initial reply, until she realized what he had said. Her head pivoted sharply to stare at him. 'I haven't kissed you!'

'Haven't you?' A wicked light flickered in his brief glance. 'That's okay, there's still time.'

'You will have a long wait for that time,' she snapped. 'In case you've forgotten, Mr. Braden, I am engaged.'

'But you're not married,' he reminded her. 'Why do you suppose your fiancé told me you were?'

An uncomfortable flush began to warm her cheeks, and she averted her face so he wouldn't see.

'I really wouldn't know,' she answered haughtily.

'Maybe he didn't feel secure enough about your affection to risk any competition?' Mitch suggested.

'Warren is very much aware of how much I love him and how eagerly I look forward to our marriage,' Susan told him in no uncertain terms.

'But to claim you were married?' An eyebrow arched with faint arrogance. 'Surely it would have been enough to admit that you were engaged.'

'Unfortunately Warren couldn't guess that you wouldn't respect the bonds of matrimony any more than an engagement ring,' she flashed.

'Hey!' he laughed softly. 'You are aiming those blows below the belt, aren't you?'

She tilted her head to the side in defiant challenge. 'I thought I was only speaking the truth.'

'You don't think much of me, do you?' drawled Mitch.

'Actually, I don't think of you at all,' she said coolly.

'Ooh———-ouch!' he smiled with a mock grimace of inflicted pain. 'Now you really are trying to upset my ego!'

'I think it's of sufficient size not to suffer any lasting harm.' Susan directed her gaze out the window at the rows of homes on the residential street. 'Our house is the two-story brick home, the second from the corner on the next block.'

Mitch Braden didn't comment as he swung the car into the driveway, stopping in front of the two-car garage. Her hand had closed over the metal door handle when her other wrist was seized.

'Will you let me go?' She looked at him coldly.

'You remind me of a racing car,' he said thoughtfully, his gaze sweeping her in absent appraisal. 'All classic design and beautiful to look at, with a lot of fire under the hood. Fire that could be amazingly responsive with the right man at the controls.'

Her pulse thudded a little faster. It was impossible to remain passive any longer and she strained to free her wrist from his firm grip. Applying only the slightest pressure, Mitch pulled her toward him.

His other hand reached out to cup the back of her neck, entangling itself in the silky curtain of her dark hair. 'You forgot to kiss me, Susan,' he said softly.

Susan forgot to struggle as the sensual line of his mouth moved closer. Then it was closing warmly over hers and her lashes fluttered down, the craziest sensation rocking her body. Almost before the kiss began, he was ending it, moving away to his own side of the car.

She blinked at him once and turned hurriedly away, opening the car door quickly, needing desperately to escape his presence. It only occurred to her when she was standing in the driveway, the car door slammed shut, that she should have slapped him for taking such liberties when he knew she was engaged.

But of course she should have offered some sort of protest, too. Slapping him after the fact would have been equal to locking the door after the house had been burglarized.

The driver's door opened and closed, too. Susan stared in disbelief when Mitch Braden walked around the car to her side.

'I am home now. You can leave any time,' she said huskily.

The grooves around his mouth deepened although he didn't actually smile. 'I promised Greg I would stick around until he came back. I think he intends to invite me to dinner. Naturally I'll accept.'

Susan breathed in sharply, ready to demand that he leave. At that same moment a car pulled into the drive. A quick glance said it was her father. Recognition of Mitch Braden was already flashing in his face, and Susan knew any hope that she would soon be rid of this man was lost.

3

An explanation why Mitch Braden had brought Susan home had been required by her father as well as an introduction. Then Susan had had to repeat the same thing again for her mother with an added word from Mitch that Greg had asked him to stay until he returned. The expected invitation to stay for dinner had immediately come from Beth Mabry.

The glitter in the blue eyes had mocked Susan's tight-lipped expression as Mitch Braden had murmured politely that he didn't want to inconvenience Mrs. Mabry before he allowed himself to be talked into staying.

It had irritated Susan, the way her mother treated him like visiting royalty. Amy hadn't been much better, practically swooning at his feet when she saw him as if he were a movie star. Her father had seemed to be the only one in her family to react normally, but then few things had ever ruffled him.

As for Susan, she had made an escape to the privacy of her room as soon as she decently could. Changing out of her office clothes, she had donned a cotton robe of cranberry red, offering a silent prayer that Warren's meeting with his father would not cancel their dinner. The alarm clock at her bedside had ticked the minutes away with infuriating slowness.

Downstairs the telephone rang. She unconsciously held her breath until her mother called, 'Susan, it's for you!'

It had to be Warren. With fingers crossed, she hurried down the stairs, the long robe swinging about her ankles. Her mother was near the base of the stairs in the living room alcove that served as an entrance hall. The phone was in her hand.

'It's Warren,' she told Susan. 'You aren't going out tonight, are you? Not with Mr. Braden staying for dinner?'

'Mitch Braden is Greg's guest, not mine,' Susan answered airily, reaching to take the receiver from her mother's hand.

Her moving gaze was caught by the man seated in the living room talking with her father. She quickly turned her back on the secretly amused gleam as she brought the telephone to her ear.

'Hello, darling,' she spoke into the mouthpiece with forced brightness.

Her greeting was not returned. Instead, Warren's harsh voice demanded, 'What did your mother just say? What was that about Mitch Braden staying for dinner?'

'That's right,' Susan breathed softly and hesitantly.

'What's he doing there?'

'I'll … I'll explain later,' she stalled.

'Does he know— Of course he knows,' Warren answered his own half-spoken question in a disgusted voice. But Susan knew what he had been going to ask, whether Mitch had learned they weren't married. 'Has he been bothering you?'

'No, of course not.' That was a lie, but the last thing Susan wanted was for Warren to make a scene. 'What about dinner this evening? Will you be free?' There was a slightly desperate ring to her voice in spite of her effort to reassure him that everything was all right.

Warren hesitated. 'Yes,' he said, then more firmly, 'Yes, I will be free. I'll be at your house in the time it takes me to drive from the office.'

'I'll be ready,' she promised, knowing that didn't give her a great deal of time.

'I'll see you, then,' he said with his usual clipped shortness, and hung up.

After Susan replaced the receiver in its cradle, her mother approached again. 'Susan—?' she began.

'Excuse me. Mom,' Susan interrupted quickly, 'but Warren is on his way here now and I don't have much time to get ready.'

Without giving her mother a chance to reply, she hurried up the stairs to her room. The cranberry-colored robe was tossed onto the bed and a classically straight dress of beige knit was taken from the clothes closet.

Dressing in record time, Susan dashed to the single bathroom on the second floor to repair her makeup. Amy was there in front of the mirror, carefully stroking her eyebrows with a tiny brush.

'Do you mind, Amy?' Susan rushed impatiently. 'I have to get ready. Warren will be here any minute.'

Her sister stepped sideways so she would be occupying only one small corner of the mirror. 'No, go ahead. You can use the mirror, too.' She set the brush in the makeup tray and picked up a tube of lip gloss.

Susan shook her head in despair and made use of her larger portion of the mirror. Sharing the bathroom with her teenage sister was something she probably should start becoming accustomed to.

'Do you think Mom would notice if I used some mascara?' Amy asked thoughtfully as she touched the corner of her mouth where some gloss had smeared.

'I'm quite sure she would,' Susan answered, hiding a smile while she remembered how impatient she had been to wear makeup.

Amy sighed and picked up the hairbrush to run it through her long auburn hair. 'He likes long hair. Did you know that?'

A tiny frown of confusion knitted her eyebrows as Susan glanced curiously at Amy's reflection in the mirror. 'Who's "he"?' she asked, retouching the light green eyeshadow.

'Mitch,' was the prompt answer. 'He asked me to call him Mitch.'

'He did?' Susan responded dryly.

'Yes.' Amy leaned forward to fluff her bangs. 'He said he had a fondness for redheads, too. Of course, he said there was nothing wrong with brunettes,' she hastened to add as if suddenly worried that Susan might have felt insulted.

'I think Mitch Braden likes women, period.' Susan added a touch of peach blusher to her cheekbones, unable to keep the sarcasm out of her voice.

'Well, women like him, so I guess that makes the feeling mutual,' Amy declared with an airy toss of her head. 'I suppose I'd better get downstairs. Mom is almost ready to put the food on the table.'

That was an understatement, Susan thought as her sister went out of the room. Mitch Braden's sex appeal seemed to know no age barriers either. Her thirteen-year-old sister had just toppled under the spell of his charm. Unless she was careful, there was no telling who might be next.

When she was finished, Susan didn't go downstairs to wait for Warren. She chose to watch for him from her bedroom window that faced the street. As soon as she saw his car drive up, she hurried downstairs to the front door, calling goodbye to her family in the dining room.

There was a chorus of answering goodbyes including Mitch Braden's mocking, 'Have a good time, Susan.'

Warren had just emerged from his car when she darted out the front door. She saw him eye the blue sports car in the driveway and the black scowl that had appeared instantaneously on his face.

'I suppose that's his car,' he commented contemptuously as he held the passenger door open for Susan.

'Yes,' she nodded.

'It's disgusting the amount of money those racing drivers win,' he muttered almost beneath his breath, closed Susan's door and walked around to the driver's side. He didn't speak again until he was behind the wheel and they were driving away from the house. 'Now tell me how you ran into that Indy man again,' he commanded.

For the third time Susan repeated the story about Greg's car breaking down and Mitch Braden's arrival to help. Then she tacked on Greg's request that Mitch wait at the house for him and her mother's subsequent invitation to dinner which was accepted.

'What did he say to you?' Warren asked when she had finished.

Susan glanced at his stern profile with some confusion. 'When?'

'When he found out about—the marriage thing?'

Taking a deep, considering breath, Susan knew she couldn't repeat Mitch's response, so she chose to lie tactfully instead.

'When he said he thought I was married, I simply told him that he had misunderstood you. That what you'd actually said was that I was to *be* your wife.'

'Good thinking.' The look in his dark eyes was almost grateful, except Warren was much too proud. 'I should have known I could count on you.'

The topic of Mitch Braden was dropped for the time being, although Susan longed to ask why Warren had lied in the beginning. Yet his name cropped up the entire evening, usually in derogatory comments made by Warren. Fortunately the blue sports car was gone when Warren brought her home.

At the office the following morning, Warren questioned her very thoroughly about what her family had told Susan concerning Mitch's visit. Since Susan had not questioned them herself, she could answer very little. She had gathered the impression that possibly Greg planned to see Mitch Braden again, but since she wasn't positive of that she didn't tell Warren.

By Saturday evening Warren seemed to have forgotten Mitch Braden's existence completely. That brought Susan considerable relief because she had been uneasy discussing him with Warren. She constantly felt she had to be on guard in case something slipped. And she didn't want to have to watch her words when she was with the man she was going to marry.

After a quiet dinner, Warren had told her that they were going to have to attend a party being given by one of his clients. Normally Susan didn't object to the mingling of business with their evenings together.

After all, when they were married, she would need to know the people Warren associated with outside of business hours. Yet tonight she had wanted them to be alone so she could be the center of his attention.

Warren had indicated they wouldn't stay long, but they had already been at Grayson Trevor's house for an hour. Susan was standing on the fringe of a group of men gathered around Warren, all of them deeply embroiled in a political discussion.

She had been with some of the younger women, but had become bored with their never-ending gossip. She had hoped to catch Warren's eye and suggest that they leave. He had seen her, but he was quite plainly not ready to leave.

Beat music was coming from the glassed veranda of the ultramodern home and Susan gravitated toward it. She stood quietly near the wall watching the rhythmic, swaying motions of the couples dancing on the tiled floor. Hidden by her long black skirt, a toe tapped in time with the music.

A young attractively dressed woman entered the room, ash blonde hair coiled in a sophisticated bun at the nape of her neck. Susan smiled in warm recognition. Anna Kemper was two years older, married with two small children. Since Susan had started dating Warren, she had met Anna at many functions such as this.

Anna spotted Susan at almost the same instant. 'Hello. Where's Warren?'

'In the other room talking politics,' she answered, smiling wryly. 'Where's Frank?'

'By now he's probably joined Warren,' Anna laughed.

'How are the children?'

Susan never learned the answer. At that moment a man came up behind her friend, his arms circling her waist. Brown hair flashed golden as the man bent his head to place a kiss in the hollow of Anna's neck. Susan's mouth opened in disbelief.

'Anna—still breathtakingly lovely, I see,' Mitch Braden murmured as he allowed the ash blonde to turn in his arms.

'Mitch!' she exclaimed gaily. 'I might have known it was you. How are you? All in one piece?'

'I'm fine,' he smiled lazily, and loosened his hold so Anna stood free. 'I can see for myself that you are, too.'

Anna turned to Susan, her hazel eyes dancing with pleasure. The words of introduction were forming on her lips, but Mitch didn't allow her to get them out.

'I knew if I looked long enough I'd find the most beautiful girl in the house,' he stated softly. 'Hello, Susan.'

'Mr. Braden.' Susan stiffly tilted her head in acknowledgment, placing emphasis on the formality of her greeting.

'Do you two know each other?' Anna asked with a frown of surprise.

'We have met,' Susan admitted in the same rigid tone, 'but I couldn't know he would be here tonight.'

29

'Didn't you know, Susan?' Mitch taunted mockingly, his eyes crinkling merrily at the corners. 'Well, listen, I'm the proverbial bad penny. I always turn up.'

'So I'm beginning to learn,' she said coolly.

'Do I dare ask,' Anna hesitated, laughing nervously, 'what the problem is between you two?'

'There isn't any problem as far as I'm concerned, but you might ask that question of Susan later when the two of you are alone,' Mitch suggested, the directness of his gaze compelling Susan to look at him. His voice became husky, losing its amused quality to become caressing. 'Dance with me, Susan.'

It was neither an order nor a question. Not even a challenge. There was a small, negative movement of her dark head.

'No, thank you,' she refused, but the firmness in her voice wavered.

He reached out and lightly closed his fingers over the wrist of one of the hands clasped in front of her. There was something very winning in the boyishly pleading tilt of his handsome face.

'What's one dance going to hurt?' he shrugged in a coaxing gesture.

'Warren——-' Susan began, glancing self-consciously over her shoulder.

'Warren isn't here.' With slight pressure, he disentangled her hands and drew her toward him. 'And while he's away, the cat is going to play—with the mouse.'

Susan cast a helpless look to Anna, seeking aid from her friend as she unresistingly allowed Mitch to lead her away. But Anna was lost in some silent speculation of her own and missed the wordless plea for help.

At the edge of the impromptu dance floor, the beat song ended and the music changed to a slow, romantic tune. 'This couldn't have worked out better if I'd planned it,' Mitch smiled slowly, and drew Susan around into his arms.

For several steps, she allowed her mind to concentrate only on following his lead. Then gradually her physical sense began to register impressions in her brain and she was unable to ignore him.

There was a clean, fresh scent about him that was definitely pleasing. His fingers were spread across the small of her back, molding her gently against him until she could feel the muscular strength in his legs and narrow hips.

She was staring at the knot of his black tie, yet she was very conscious of the strong-columned throat and the width of his shoulders beneath the black evening suit. The caressing warmth of his breath was near her temple. There seemed to be a steady increase in the rate of her heartbeat.

Her hand stiffened against his shoulder in protest to the way he was affecting her. 'Would you please not hold me so close?' she requested lowly.

'Why not?' he asked in the same low tone that sounded disturbingly sensual at these close quarters.

'Because it isn't right,' Susan answered, trying to breathe normally.

There was a testing movement of his hand on her back. 'It feels right,' murmured Mitch.

'Well, it doesn't look right,' she replied in an almost desperate whisper.

He tipped his head downward, his mouth moving against her dark hair as he spoke. 'To whom?'

'To everyone.' Her heart was thudding against her ribs, a traitorous weakness flowing into her limbs. She glanced wildly around the room, pulling away from the warm breath that teased the hair at her temples, but only Anna appeared to be watching them. 'Mitch, please don't do that.'

A finger touched her chin to draw her gaze back to his face. There was no laughing curve in his mouth. The bronze tan of his cheeks, smoothly shaven from cheekbone to jawline, invited her caress. The teasing glitter was absent from his eyes, but their darkening blue fire made Susan feel warm all over.

'Do you have any idea how long I've been waiting to hear you say my name?'

'I——.' Susan faltered. No man should be so handsome! His gaze became riveted on her lips and she couldn't think straight.

'This is a fine time to be in the middle of a dance floor, isn't it, darling?' A faint, dry smile curved his mouth.

She breathed in sharply. 'Don't call me that!'

'Why not?' he asked complacently. 'That's the way I think of you. Honey, darling——'

'Stop it!' Susan quickly lowered her gaze to the white of his shirt collar. 'You forget I'm engaged.'

'I haven't forgotten.'

'Then would you please leave me alone!' she protested, filled with a strange anger that she didn't understand.

'Do you mean here, right this minute?' A quick glance revealed his expression was serious in spite of the teasing lightness in his voice.

Susan looked around at the other couples, knowing eyebrows would rise if she and Mitch parted company in the middle of a song. Her wandering gaze was caught by Warren standing in the veranda doorway. His withdrawn expression was cold with displeasure. At that moment Anna approached Warren and Susan's gaze was released.

She swung it back to the black cloth of Mitch's jacket. 'Warren is here,' she muttered nervously.

'Am I supposed to quake in my shoes?' he asked in an amused tone.

'Oh, Mitch, would you be serious?' Susan demanded impatiently.

'Believe me, I'm very serious.'

She let the double meaning of his comment sail over her head. 'I don't want there to be any trouble.'

'You, mean that you don't want any fights started,' Mitch defined. 'Most women would feel complimented to have two men coming to blows over them.'

'I wouldn't, so please don't ... don't rile him.'

'Are you afraid I might get hurt?'

She had felt the sinewy strong muscles in his chest, arms and thighs. Warren might have a weight advantage, but Mitch Braden was in much better physical condition.

Susan shook her head. 'I just don't want any trouble.'

'I wouldn't worry,' Mitch replied. 'Your fiancé is an attorney. He fights with words.'

'And you believe that actions speak louder?'

He shrugged indifferently. 'Let's just say that former opponents have indicated that I'm experienced with both.'

There was little doubt in her mind that he spoke the truth. She remembered the first meeting when his mock-serious comments had demolished Warren's composure to the point that he had lied about his and Susan's being married.

'Please, Mitch, don't start anything, for my sake,' Susan requested humbly.

The glint of humor left his gaze as it traveled over her upturned face. His solemn expression made her suddenly aware of an unrelenting quality in his handsome features. Beneath the surface charm and roguish air was a man of iron determination, incapable of wavering once he had set his mind on a goal.

'You have my word,' he answered evenly, 'for this once.'

And Susan knew instinctively that Mitch would keep his promise. She breathed an inaudible sigh of relief and smiled. A corner of his mouth quirked in response.

Their steps automatically ceased as the last note of the song faded. The lull in the music made Susan aware of the voices and laughter that filled the house.

The smile left her face before she turned to make her way toward Warren, Mitch's arm curved lightly across her back for his hand to rest on the side of her waist. The light possession was removed when they reached Warren.

'Hello, Warren.' Susan smiled with an attempt at naturalness as she moved to his side and slipped a hand beneath his elbow. His dark eyes gave her a sense of guilt even though she knew she had done nothing wrong.

'Susan,' he acknowledged, her with a cool smile.

'I've returned her to you safe and unharmed, Mr. Sullivan,' Mitch commented, inclining his head with mock condescension.

'Thank you, Mr. Braden.' Susan could feel Warren's tense anger.

'And thank you for the dance, Miss Mabry.' Cynical laughter glittered in the blue eyes that were turned to her. 'Is that polite enough for you?'

'Y—you're quite welcome,' Susan acknowledged before glancing anxiously at the puckering frown of confusion in Warren's face.

'Forgive me, Mr. Sullivan,' Mitch apologized. 'Susan has been giving me a lesson in manners.'

A black brow arched inquiringly at Susan, the imposing arrogance of Warren's stance commanding her attention. Then his dark gaze slid back to Mitch Braden.

'I hope you didn't find it too difficult to learn,' he offered complacently.

'It wasn't easy to accept, Mr. Sullivan, believe me,' responded Mitch, dry-voiced. He glanced to Anna and her husband Frank Kemper. 'Anna, Frank,' he greeted them with a nod of his head. 'Excuse me, won't you? I think I'll go find the refreshment bar.'

With that Mitch moved away, walking lightly on the balls of his feet like an athlete. An uneasy silence followed his departure, one that neither Susan nor the couple standing next to her were willing to break.

'How did he succeed in crashing the party?' Warren muttered, staring after Mitch.

Frank Kemper ran a hand through his curling brown hair, hiding the glitter of amusement that appeared briefly in his brown eyes. 'I would guess he came with the Colesons. Their son is one of his chief mechanics and design engineers.'

'Are you acquainted with him, Frank?' Warren glanced curiously at his friend.

'Yes, although actually he's more Anna's friend than mine.'

The reply had Warren arching a brow of surprise at Frank's ash blonde wife. Anna glanced hesitantly at her husband as if asking him just how she should explain before replying.

'Mitch and I grew up in the same small town in Michigan. Of course, he's older than I am, but our parents were always good friends. We've been more or less like cousins,' Anna concluded.

'I see,' Warren drawled.

But Susan wasn't certain if she did. That hadn't been exactly a cousinly kiss Anna had received on the neck from Mitch. At the same time they had been more than cousins. Susan didn't have time to consider the thought further as Warren claimed her attention.

'I certainly hope you put him in his place once and for all,' he said.

'I doubt if anyone could do that,' Anna commented. 'That's supposing Mitch Braden had a place.'

Susan agreed, but she did so silently.

'Are you ready to leave, Susan?' Warren's hand closed possessively over the slender fingers resting on his arm.

'Yes, if you are.' She glanced into his face, seeing that the remoteness and coldness were gone. The ardent light in his dark eyes said she was forgiven for whatever it was that she had done wrong.

'I am,' he smiled, his rugged features possessing a wondrous softness with the action.

'So soon?' Anna sighed, then smiled understandingly at the engaged couple. 'Very well, I'll walk with Susan while she gets her coat.'

'I won't be long,' Susan promised Warren before leaving to get her wrap. As she and Anna left the glassed veranda for the main living area of the house, she took a deep, calming breath. 'You never did tell me how the children were.'

'And you never did tell me how you met Mitch.' A pair of hazel eyes twinkled back.

Susan paused for a second. 'It isn't a pleasant memory.'

'I can't believe that,' her friend laughed shortly. 'Tell me about it.'

After relating an accurate version of the first encounter in the restaurant, Susan tacked on a shortened version of Mitch stopping to aid them on the highway. She didn't know why she hadn't refused to discuss it with Anna.

'No wonder Warren was livid with jealousy when he saw you dancing with him,' Anna declared with decided amusement. 'Only Mitch would walk up to a total stranger and tell him how beautiful he thinks the man's date is.'

'Since you know him, I wish you'd tell him to leave me alone,' Susan sighed.

'Does he bother you?'

'It's embarrassing to have him following me around. I mean, I'm engaged.'

'Don't ask me to believe you don't find him attractive,' Anna smiled widely. 'No woman is immune to his looks and charm.'

Susan tipped her head to the side, gazing at her friend with curious speculation. 'Including you, Anna?'

Nonplussed, the blonde glanced away. 'That's a question that requires a delicately phrased answer from a married woman like myself. I'm not immune to Mitch,' she sighed ruefully. 'He can still make me feel like I'm very much a woman, but not in that special way that Frank does. I'm very much in love with my husband and I wouldn't trade him for anyone else even if I could.'

'But you and Mitch were more than just make-believe cousins once?' Susan voiced the impression she had received earlier.

They entered the guest room being used as a powder room for the party that evening. Susan paused near one of the mirrors, waiting for the response to her half-statement and half-question. Anna lowered her voice so she couldn't be over-heard by the other chattering women in the room.

'There was a time,' she acknowledged, frankly meeting Susan's gaze, 'when I was very much infatuated with Mitch. I could have easily fallen in love with him if I'd received the slightest encouragement. But he let me down easy, never once hurting my feelings or damaging our friendship.'

Guilty at having pried into something that was none of her business, Susan looked away. 'I'm sorry, Anna. I had no right to ask that. You should have told me not to be so nosy.'

'I don't mind.' Anna shook her head, absently watching as Susan retrieved her spring coat. 'Mitch has been racing for several years now. Well, actually he's been racing cars since he was in high school, but only in the last few years has he been winning consistently. With his looks and personality, the press automatically tagged him as the bachelor playboy of the circuit. But he isn't a shallow person, Susan. He's very warm and very sincere and very intelligent. Frank says Mitch has an uncanny knack for making the right investment and a very astute business mind.'

'Why are you telling me all this?' Susan frowned.

'Because ...' Anna shrugged uncertainly, 'because of the attention he's paying you, I guess.'

'I'm flattered, of course, but———'

Anna interrupted. 'What I'm really saying is that if I'd received the encouragement you have, I'd already be in love with him.'

Nervously Susan turned away, her fingers fidgeting with the lining of her coat. 'You're forgetting that I'm already in love with Warren and we're going to be married in August.'

'Yes, I suppose I was,' the other girl agreed with self-conscious brightness. 'Speaking of Warren, he's probably worried that Mitch has waylaid you somewhere.'

Draping the light coat over her arm, Susan turned, an equally false smile on her face. She didn't like the vague stirrings of uneasiness she felt.

'We'd better be getting back,' she nodded.

As the two girls retraced their path to the veranda, Susan spied Mitch standing in the far corner of a room talking with two men. His gaze flicked to her at almost the same instant. There was an almost imperceptible nod of his head to acknowledge her look but no flashing smile to make her heart quicken.

When Susan walked through the room again at Warren's side, she refused to let her gaze be drawn to that corner of the room. Mitch Braden was physically attractive, but there was room for only one man in her life and that was Warren. She didn't intend to complicate things by encouraging Mitch, however unconsciously.

In the car she snuggled close to Warren, needing his nearness to chase away the shivers of apprehension that danced over her skin. When the car was started and they were on the road, he slid his arm around her shoulders and nestled her closer.

'Love me, Susan?' he asked, taking his attention from the road long enough to brush a kiss against the side of her hair.

'You know I do, darling,' she answered fervently, and wondered why she was so desperate to convince Warren of the fact.

4

Warren bent over Susan's desk, adding the typed notes she had given him to the stack of papers clipped together in his hand. He barely glanced at her as he issued instructions with a preoccupied air. 'I shall probably be with my father all afternoon. Hold all my calls unless Con Anderson phones. Put him straight through,' he ordered crisply.

'I will,' Susan acknowledged.

Warren straightened. 'I'm beginning to look forward to my father entering the hospital tomorrow.' A sardonic smile lifted the corners of his mouth. 'Maybe the office will settle into some semblance of routine again.'

A faint, agreeing smile appeared briefly on her lips, but Warren was already gathering his papers together and starting for the hall door.

Susan sighed and glanced at the small desk calendar. A silent prayer of thanks was offered that the three-day Memorial weekend was only two days away. She would welcome the time to recover from this hectic pace that seemed to require a constant juggling of appointments and schedules.

The hall door closed behind Warren as Susan swiveled to her typewriter, reaching for the earpiece of the dictaphone. The ringing of the telephone checked her movement.

'Warren Sullivan's office,' Susan answered in her courteous, professional voice.

'Hello, Beautiful,' was the immediate response.

Susan froze, unable to breathe or speak. It couldn't possibly be Mitch Braden. He would never call her at work, would he?

'Did you wish to speak to Mr. Sullivan?' she asked coolly.

'Hardly,' Mitch chuckled.

The hall door opened and Susan quickly placed her hand over the receiver mouthpiece as Warren strode into her office. 'Forgot my notepad,' he said in explanation, walking to her desk and retrieving the legal size pad of yellow paper. He glanced at the telephone in her hand. 'Is that for me? Find out who it is. I might not be in.'

'No,' she said hurriedly. 'It's for me.' A curious light entered Warren's dark eyes. It was a rarity for Susan to receive a personal call at the office. 'It's … it's my mother,' she lied. 'She wants me to pick up some things at the store on my way home.'

With a satisfied nod, he turned to the hall door. 'Give her my regards,' he tossed over his shoulder absently.

Susan let out the deep breath she had been holding and slipped her hand away from the mouthpiece of the telephone. She didn't speak until the door was firmly closed behind Warren and she heard his footsteps echoing down the outside hall.

'What was it you wanted, Mr. Braden? I'm very busy,' she inquired with cool hauteur.

His tongue clicked reprovingly in her ear. 'Lying to your boss is one thing, Susan, but lying to your fiancé? Shame on you!' he mocked.

An embarrassed red warmed her neck. 'If you've merely called to ——-' she began angrily.

'To invite you on a guided tour of the race grounds tonight,' Mitch interrupted lazily, 'with a stop for dinner afterward.'

"I'm busy.'

'Tomorrow night isn't possible, I know,' he said with remarkable indifference to her sharp tone. 'Tuesday, Thursday, Saturday and Sunday nights are when you have your appointments with Warren.'

'They're dates,' Susan corrected.

'All right, they're dates,' Mitch conceded. 'Now, when are you and I going to have a date? It's been four days since I saw you last. Haven't you missed me?'

'Was I supposed to?' The coldness of her voice was to help freeze away the image of his handsome face that kept trying to dance into her mind.

'I hoped you would,' he replied with a warm huskiness in his voice that made his words almost a physical caress. Susan swallowed, trying to ease the tightness in her throat. Her pulse was skipping erratically. 'I want to see you tonight, Susan. I promise I'll be a good little boy.'

'I told you, I'm busy,' she hurried, feeling the pull of his masculine attraction even over the telephone lines. 'I have to wash my hair and———'

'Can't you think of anything more original?' his amused voice laughed in her ear. 'No man believes that excuse any more.'

'You're right,' Susan said with sudden determination. 'I don't need to make excuses. I won't go out with you tonight or any other night, Mitch. I'm engaged to be married.'

There was a short pause before he responded in a quiet voice. 'Is that your final word?'

A muscle constricted painfully in her chest. 'Yes,' she answered, trying to ignore the hurt.

'Okay,' Mitch sighed, reluctantly accepting her reply. 'Maybe I'll see you around some time,' he said in a shrugging tone that indicated he doubted the possibility. 'So long, Beautiful.'

'Goodbye, Mitch.'

Something seemed to be burning her eyes as she hung up the telephone receiver. Nervously she ran a shaking hand through her dark silken hair, and blinked rapidly.

Drat the man! Why had he bothered to call? He must have known she would refuse to go out with him. And she had just begun to convince herself that she had heard the last of him. In fact she had even started to forget about him, at least partially, until this telephone call.

Why had she talked to him? she asked herself angrily. She should have hung up the phone the instant she recognized his voice. Or why hadn't she told Warren who was on the phone and let him deal with Mitch?

Since the first time she had met him, Mitch Braden had been disrupting her life, her senses, her emotions, and her relationship with Warren. She wanted to feel the peace and contentment she had known before she met him. Every time she thought she was about to obtain it, Mitch Braden popped up again, disrupting things all over again.

Now he had even confused her to the point where she was sorry that she would never see him again. What was worse, she seemed powerless to stop the sadness from invading her heart.

It was a good thing she wouldn't be seeing or hearing from him again. And it was a good thing that the race would be run this weekend and Mitch Braden would be leaving town within a few days after its conclusion.

Without him around to disrupt her, her life would settle into its previous pattern. The ripples his unexpected arrival had brought into her tranquil life would eventually disappear, without leaving any mark.

The logic didn't cheer Susan.

Her dark hair was caught in saucy pigtails on either side of her head, secured with ribbons of mint green to match the thin fabric of her short-sleeved polka-dot blouse. The wide legs of her white slacks swung about her ankles as she walked down the hospital corridor with Warren, the raised heels of her sandals clicking loudly in the hushed building.

'I told Father we might stop in this afternoon after our picnic,' said Warren. 'He's been waiting for me to bring you each time I've come to see him. I would have suggested it before, of course, except that the doctor thought it would be best to keep visitors at an absolute minimum the first couple of days after the operation.'

'I thought you said the operation took less time than expected and that your father had come through it in excellent shape,' Susan frowned.

'He did, but with his advanced years, it was still a shock to his system. We didn't want to take any risks of complication,' he explained. 'Here's his room.'

He indicated a door ahead and to Susan's right. She waited for him to open it, then walked into the semiprivate room. Robert Sullivan was partially sitting up in his bed, wire-rimmed glasses perched on the end of his nose. He looked over the top of them and closed the magazine on his lap. He looked pale but otherwise in good health.

'Hello, Susan.' He extended his hand toward her and she walked to the side of his bed to accept its firm clasp. 'You certainly are the picture of a summer's day!'

Blinking once in surprise at the rare compliment from the usually taciturn man, Susan smiled. 'Thank you. You're looking quite fit, too. How are you?'

'Stiff, sore, and uncomfortable, but that's to be expected I guess,' he replied, releasing her hand and turning to his son 'Hello, Warren.'

Susan knew she had been dismissed and moved from the side of the bed to an armchair that stood near the foot. The partitioning curtain was drawn, concealing the second occupant of the hospital room, although the loud playing of a radio from the other side made Susan doubt that the patient would possibly be sleeping.

'That radio is awfully loud, isn't it?' Warren frowned in the direction of the curtain.

'Yes,' his father sighed heavily. 'I wish he'd turn the volume down.'

'Would you like me to ask him to do it?'

'No, no.' Robert Sullivan impatiently waved aside the offer. 'The man's half deaf. He can't hear it if he turns it any lower. Besides, I've already told him I didn't object. He doesn't have it on very often.'

With that explanation, Warren's father shifted the conversation to an article he had just been reading concerning a supreme court decision recently made. Susan wondered if he had any interest outside of his profession.

It didn't really matter, she decided, glancing at Warren and smiling to herself. They had had a wonderful time on their picnic. Warren had brought along a bottle of wine to go with the meal she had packed. He had taken her to a secluded spot alongside the rapids of a river. The setting had been idyllic, just the two of them alone, talking about their plans for the future.

Susan had been so contented lying on the blanket in his arms. She had hated it when they had to leave. Yet the rosy afterglow of the moment was still with her, maybe the aftereffects of the wine she had drunk.

Leaning back in her seat, Susan relaxed, not minding now that she wasn't the sole object of Warren's attention. From the other side of the curtain, the radio dial was turned, jumbling music together until it was finally stopped to the sound of a radio announcer's words.

'And now we'll go trackside with Jim Jensen and a report on the status of the Indianapolis 500.'

There was a roar in the background, followed by a second man's voice. 'Hello, ladies and gentlemen, this is Jim Jensen. Let me bring you up to date on the Indy 500. It will be no surprise to you racing fans out there when I say that the leader is none other than Mitch Braden.'

Susan clenched her teeth in frustration at the sound of his name. She wanted to rush over there and turn off that radio. The mention of the man's name seemed to destroy her contentment.

'He's been leading the pack since almost the beginning of the race,' the radio announcer continued.

'The first hundred miles Braden and another veteran driver, Johnny Phelps, jockeyed for the lead before Braden took command. He's been leading by a comfortable margin ever since.'

Trying to close her ears to the man's voice, Susan concentrated on the rainbow colors flashing from her diamond engagement ring. But her hearing seemed to grow more acute.

'The yellow caution flag has only been out three times. Except for those three minor mishaps, the race has been free of accidents. Twelve cars are out with mechanical malfunctions, but none of the drivers of those twelve cars were expected to be among the front runners today.

'If Mitch Braden does receive the checkered flag today,' the announcer's voice raised slightly as the background roar of racing engines grew louder, 'he's going to have to give a lot of credit to the outstanding performance of his pit crew today. They've been phenomenal. I say that because I see Braden

41

is heading into the pits now. Let's take a few seconds to time him, and ladies and gentlemen, with that crew, a few seconds is all it's going to be.'

Suddenly the pitch of the man's voice changed. 'Braden is in the pits, slowing— An accident! In the pits!' Susan's eyes widened in alarm. 'It happened so fast! Braden was coming in, just starting to slow down, when Mark Terry, who was well back in the pack, accelerated out of his pit area. He couldn't have seen Braden coming in! His car ran right into the side of Braden's and rolled up on top of it!'

Her heart was in her throat, all the blood leaving her limbs until she felt chilled to the bone. It couldn't be happening! It wasn't really true!

'Terry has scrambled out of his car, seemingly unharmed, but there's no sign of Braden!' The announcer continued his eyewitness account in a fever-pitched tone. 'Emergency vehicles are already on the scene and I can see the familiar blue uniforms of Braden's pit crew. I don't see any sign of fire, but it's impossible to be certain. If Braden is trapped underneath Terry's car———' The thought wasn't finished, to Susan's horror, her imagination working much too vividly.

'I can see men working frantically on one side of Braden's car now! Yes, yes, they're pulling him out! He doesn't appear to be conscious. But of course we can't know how seriously he's been injured. That finishes the race for Braden, though. Johnny Phelps is the new leader. What a tough break, fans! They have Braden on a stretcher and are loading him into the ambulance. The Indy officials can be proud of the speed with which the rescue men reacted. I———'

'Susan. Susan?' Warren's frowning voice broke sharply in.

'Wh—what?' She looked at him blankly.

'You're as white as a sheet.' He walked swiftly to her side. 'Are you ill? What's the matter with you?'

She did feel sick. Her hands were cold and clammy when Warren clasped them firmly in his own. A black nausea was swimming before her eyes.

'I—I think I need a breath of—of fresh air,' she stammered. How could she possibly explain her reaction to the news of Mitch's accident? It didn't make sense to be so violently upset simply because she knew him.

Warren helped her to stand. 'Would you want me to go with you?'

'No.' Her knees were shaking badly as she shook her head in denial. 'I'll be all right in a moment, really. It's just a little stuffy in here. Ex—excuse me, please.'

Her rounded brown eyes bounced away from Warren's concerned gaze and she barely caught the frowning look from Robert Sullivan. She managed to force her legs to carry her into the hallway. Out of sight of the door, she leaned weakly against the corridor wall, breathing in deeply to quell the churning of her stomach.

The long gulps of air seemed to breathe strength into her limbs. The nameless terror that gripped her heart started to ease as her knees stopped their quivering.

'Susan?' Warren stood beside her, his eyes anxiously examining the pallor that remained in her face.

'You needn't have come.' She took another deep breath. 'I'm sorry I——'

'Don't apologize,' he interrupted, circling an arm under her shoulders and drawing her away from the wall. 'Let's get you outside in the fresh air.'

'I'm all right, really,' she protested weakly, but she let his strength carry her along. 'I just felt a little faint there for a moment.'

'Maybe it was the wine,' Warren suggested with a gentle smile.

'Yes,' she breathed, taking advantage of the excuse he offered.

The late spring air did its reviving act, returning color to her cheeks. The shock of Mitch's accident had dissipated, but a feeling of sick dread remained. When Warren suggested taking her home, she made only a halfhearted protest.

'Your father——-' she began.

'——-will understand perfectly. I'll call in to see him on my way to pick you up this evening, providing you're feeling fit enough to go out,' he said, helping her into his car. His solicitude made her feel even more guilty for not telling him the real cause of her upset state.

When they had driven out of the hospital parking lot, Susan glanced hesitantly at his carved profile. 'Do you mind if—if we turn the radio on?'

'Of course not.' He smiled at her crookedly, a frown of curious confusion drawing his dark brows together as he reached out to switch on the radio.

A news broadcast was on and Warren started to turn the dial to some music. 'No,' Susan rushed to stop him. 'That station is fine.'

Warren shrugged and left it there. Crossing her fingers in her lap that the news hadn't been on very long, Susan listened to a synopsis of the world news and swallowed when the announcer changed to the local scene.

Forcing a stoic expression into her face, she listened to a shortened account of the accident minus the terrorizing adjectives. A cautious glance at Warren caught him listening interestedly, too.

'—We do not have a report on the extent or seriousness of the injuries to Mitch Braden,' the announcer said. 'An ambulance attendant did say that Braden had regained consciousness in the ambulance. When we have more information, we'll pass it on to you.'

Susan's lashes fluttered down in temporary relief.

'Well, our Indy man seems to have had some bad luck,' Warren commented dryly.

Susan winced. 'Don't be flippant, Warren, please!'

43

'I didn't mean to sound callous.' He slid a questioning look in her direction. 'I may not like the man, but I certainly wouldn't wish him any crippling injury.'

Her heart catapulted into her throat. She hadn't considered the possibility that Mitch might be maimed or paralyzed. Her initial fear had been for his life. The prospect of that vital, handsome man chained to crutches or a wheelchair or a bed sent more sickening chills over her skin.

'I know you don't, Warren,' she replied, suppressing a shudder.

She leaned her head against the back cushion of her seat, closing her eyes and trying to achieve the indifferent interest Warren displayed.

'We'll be at your home shortly,' he said, misinterpreting her action and wanness as another sign of the dizziness she had suffered in the hospital and not connecting it with Mitch Braden's accident.

Soft music from the radio filled the silence. The soothing melody didn't penetrate Susan's thoughts, however. Her mind was replaying the last conversation she had had on the telephone with Mitch. She had been so sharp and so cold with him.

It hurt unbearably now to think that those might have been the last words she would exchange with him. She could have gotten the same message across with politeness and humor instead of being so indignant and rude.

The motion of the car stopped. Susan blinked her eyes open, recognizing the gracefully old brick home, and swung her head to look into Warren's dark eyes. He was half-turned in his seat, studying her quietly, his arm resting along the top of the cushion near her head.

With his forefinger, he reached out to touch the tuft of dark hair held by the green ribbon. 'You look more like a little girl who's had too many treats at the fair than a woman who's had too much wine,' he mused, then tilted his jet black head in concern. 'Are you sure you're going to be all right?'

'I'll be fine,' she smiled stiffly.

'You wait here,' Warren ordered, 'while I get the picnic hamper from the back.'

Susan did as she was told, remaining in the car until his supporting hand helped her out and guided her to the front door of her home. Only when they were inside did Warren release his hold.

'Oh, Susan, it's you!' Her mother appeared in the hallway, from the direction of the kitchen, wiping her hands on a towel. 'I didn't expect you home so soon.'

'Susan isn't feeling well, Mrs. Mabry,' said Warren.

'It's nothing, Mom, really,' Susan murmured quickly as Beth Mabry walked forward with concern in her brown eyes.

'You do look a bit pale, dear.' She pressed a hand against Susan's cheek. 'You don't seem to have a temperature, though.'

44

'You two are making a fuss about nothing.' Susan tried to laugh. 'It's just a little headache and dizziness. If I lay down for an hour it will go away.'

'I'll call you about six-thirty to see if you feel up to going out tonight,' Warren stated. 'If she isn't feeling better in an hour or so, Mrs. Mabry, I hope you'll have your husband take a look at her.'

'I will,' Beth Mabry promised. 'Let me take that picnic hamper for you, Warren. And Susan, you go and lie down.'

'You do as she tells you,' Warren added, touching Susan's cheek with his hand in a goodbye caress.

Susan stared at the front door for several seconds after Warren had closed it, wishing that she could have shared some of the anxiety she was feeling with him. But he wouldn't have understood. For that matter she didn't understand it very well herself.

'Would you like an aspirin or something, Susan?' Beth Mabry watched the unusual melancholy emotions flitting across her daughter's face.

'No, nothing,' Susan refused absently, and started toward the stairwell leading to the second floor.

A car pulled into the drive, the sound followed immediately by the slamming of doors and footsteps approaching the front door. Susan turned toward it, her hand poised on the banister. Her brother walked into the house ahead of his father. Greg's chin was tucked into his chest, hands shoved in his pockets and shoulders hunched forward.

In Susan's shock and subsequent worry, she had completely forgotten that Mitch had mailed complimentary tickets to the race today and that her father and brother had attended.

'Simon?' her mother exclaimed with some surprise. 'Is the race over already?'

'No,' he replied, glancing with concern at his son's bowed head. 'There was an accident at the track. Mitch Braden has been taken to the hospital.'

'No!' Her mother's denial was given in astonishment and fear.

Amy appeared at the top of the stairs, a hairbrush in her hand. 'Mitch is hurt?'

'I'm afraid so, kitten,' her father affirmed grimly, and Susan noticed the tightness of his mouth.

For all his outward control, Simon Mabry was upset, too. In his short acquaintanceship, Mitch Braden had managed to touch all their lives.

'Was it ... was it very bad?' her mother asked in a voice barely above a whisper. Susan guessed that she was envisaging a flaming crash and remembered her own surge of terror at that imagined picture. 'Is he seriously hurt?'

'It was bad enough,' Simon answered. 'He was trapped for a short time under another car. We heard a radio report on the way home that he had regained consciousness before reaching the hospital, but nothing about any injuries.'

'If something happens to him,' Amy wailed, 'I'll just die!'

45

Greg shifted his feet uncomfortably and Susan wanted to walk over and put an arm around his shoulders to say that she felt the same miserable pain he did. Fear of the unknown was eating at her heart, too.

'I think I'll turn on the radio,' he mumbled. 'Maybe they'll know something else.'

'Wait a minute, son,' Simon laid a hand on Greg's shoulder. 'Maybe I can cut through some of the red tape.'

'What are you going to do, Daddy?' Amy raced down the steps past Susan, the long auburn hair that Mitch had professed to like shimmering like fire.

'I'm going to call emergency receiving and see if I can't find out something,' he answered in a decisive tone.

Susan gasped back the little sob that tried to escape and followed the others as they hurried after her striding doctor father. In the study, they all huddled around the desk where her father sat.

'I think Kate Johnson has the duty today,' he mused absently and flipped through his telephone list for the hospital number. 'She's an excellent surgeon,' he told them as he dialed the number.

It seemed an interminable time before anyone answered.

'This is Doctor Simon Mabry', her father identified himself. 'I'd like to speak to Doctor Johnson.' There was another pause, filled by the drumming of her father's fingers on the desk top. 'Kate? Simon Mabry here. What? ... No, no, I'm not bringing anyone in. I was calling about Mitch Braden, the race car driver they brought in from the speedway ... I guessed that, but can you give me what you've got?'

Studying her father's expression intently, Susan didn't move, but waited motionless like the rest of her family. He listened quietly to the woman doctor on the other end of the phone, his silence occasionally punctuated by his grunts of understanding.

'Thank you, Kate,' he said finally. 'I appreciate this.' Then he said goodbye and hung up.

'Well?' Susan probed anxiously.

'So far,' he breathed in deeply, lifting his head to meet the gazes centered on him, 'they know he has a broken arm, some cracked ribs, and a concussion. They're still checking for internal injuries and the like.'

A sigh of relief seemed to come from all of them. Susan only knew she wanted to cry, her knees buckling slightly before stiffening to support her.

'I knew all the time he would be all right,' Amy declared brightly.

'He's tough,' Greg agreed with a tight smile, man-fully trying to conceal his emotions.

'I'm so relieved.' Beth Mabry shook her head as if astounded to discover how tense she had been. 'Every year you hear about a crash of some sort in the Indianapolis 500, but this is the first time we've ever known anyone involved, as more than just a name, I mean.'

'I think we all understand, Beth.' Simon Mabry glanced warmly about him at the smiling, relieved faces of his children.

Susan swallowed the tight lump in her throat and turned away from the group. Her fingers were still pressed against her stomach, but the nauseous churning had stopped. Mitch was going to be all right, said a joyous voice from her heart.

'Susan, in all the excitement,' her mother exclaimed, 'I forgot you were supposed to be resting.'

'Resting?' her father questioned. 'Aren't you feeling well, Susan?'

'I—I had a headache,' she answered self-consciously, not quite meeting her parents' eyes. 'It seems to have gone away, though.'

Which was the truth.

'With all the distraction, you probably forgot to feel ill,' her mother smiled. 'Warren was certainly worried. He'll be glad to hear you're all right.'

'Yes,' Susan agreed, with a faint answering smile.

Now that she was feeling better there was no reason not to go out with him that evening. But the dinner was an anticlimax. Susan couldn't seem to recapture the peace and contentment she had experienced earlier in his company.

Warren naturally blamed her restlessness on the lingering effect of her headache, and Susan let him, since she couldn't explain to herself why she couldn't find that previous sensation of closeness to him.

5

Nervously adjusting the collar of her peach-colored jacket, Susan paused in the hospital corridor. Her palm was faintly damp and she pressed it against her skirt before clutching the leather case a little tighter. Her gaze darted swiftly into the open doorways of the hospital rooms in the hall as she started forward again.

'May I help you, miss?' a female voice inquired behind her.

Susan turned with a start, smiling self-consciously. 'No,' she answered quickly, glancing at the leather case in her hands. 'I was just bringing some papers to Mr. Robert Sullivan.'

The uniformed nurse, an older woman with beautiful waving white hair and twinkling eyes, smiled and nodded. 'His room is three doors down to your right.'

'Thank you,' Susan turned away, her moving gaze flicking to the open doorway on the opposite side of the hall. There was a rustle of movement from the room.

'Hey, Beautiful! Is that you?' Mitch Braden's voice rang clearly into the hall.

A red blush of embarrassment filled Susan's face as she turned instinctively toward the door in answer and caught the amused, raised eyebrow of the nurse.

Her step hesitated for only a second before she continued to the room. She told herself she wouldn't stay more than a couple of minutes, just pop in to wish him a polite get-well.

'Susan?' his inquiring voice called again as she walked through the open door of his hospital room.

He didn't see her immediately. He was trying to push himself into a more upright position in the bed with one arm. There was a wince of pain and his face went pale before he slumped back.

'Lie still,' Susan ordered quickly, walking swiftly to his bedside.

The blue eyes opened and Mitch simply looked at her for a long moment. 'Hello,' he said softly, lean dimples appearing in the tanned cheeks.

Her chest constricted at the dark glow in his eyes. 'Hello,' she returned with equal softness, a faint smile on her mouth.

'I heard your voice in the hall.' His compelling gaze refused to let her look away. 'I didn't think you would come in to see me.'

'What were you going to do?' she teased gently. 'Come racing after me?'

There was an urge to reach out and smooth the tousled gold-brown hair falling across his forehead. Susan moved away from the bed before she succumbed to it.

'I might have. My legs weren't injured, only this,' Mitch tapped the cast on his left arm, 'and a few ribs and a bump on the head.'

'The last certainly didn't knock any sense into you!' She let her hand trail over the foot of the bed and close over the rail, balancing the leather case containing the papers for Robert Sullivan beside it.

'Did you think it might?'

She could feel his eyes watching her. The intentness of his gaze began to affect her breathing and she shifted uncomfortably. Somehow the conversation had become too intimate. She had intended only to make an aloof, polite inquiry about his health, and here she was trading a kind of soft banter with him.

'I don't know,' she shrugged, and stared at the diamond ring on her wedding finger.

'Well!' Mitch breathed in. 'Have I lost track of time? Isn't this Tuesday? Shouldn't you be working?'

Her glance was almost grateful at his change of subject, 'It's Tuesday and I'm working. Warren's father is here in the hospital recovering from an operation. I was bringing him some papers to study.'

'I see.' He paused. 'Were you at the race? I looked for you, but I only saw your father and Greg. I sent enough tickets.'

'Yes, I know you did,' Susan answered nervously. 'I know they would want me to thank you for them too. Warren and I had already made plans to go on a picnic.'

A wry smile tugged the corners of his mouth. 'It's probably just as well the two of you weren't there. Warren would probably have cheered when he saw the crash.'

'That's not fair,' she protested. 'All of us were upset when we heard about the accident.'

'Were you?' He shot her a piercing blue look.

Susan glanced away, afraid he might have some way of getting inside her mind and finding out how upset she had been. 'Of course,' she answered curtly. Tossing her head back, she let go of the railing and hugged the leather case in front of her. 'I really have to be going, Mitch. Mr. Sullivan is expecting me. I … I hope you're feeling better soon.'

'Wait.' His voice checked her movement toward the door. She glanced warily over her shoulder. 'You haven't autographed my cast yet.' He flashed her a smile that made her heart turn over.

Susan hesitated as she watched Mitch reach for a black pen lying on the table beside his bed. With a resigned sigh she walked back to the bed, taking the pen he extended toward her. The briefcase was awkwardly in the way and she set it on the bed. She bent slightly over him, the pen poised above the cast as she tried to decide what to write.

'You could put down "All my love" or "Love and kisses"' Mitch suggested with a twinkle.

As quickly as the pen and cast would allow, Susan scrawled 'Get well soon' and signed her name. Straightening, she held the pen out to him, reaching for the case with her other hand. But instead of taking the pen, his right hand took hold of hers.

'Susan?' Her startled eyes met his faintly earnest gaze that searched her face. 'I would like you to come see me again,' he said, almost humbly.

'I'm afraid that's not possible.' She tried to withdraw her hand, but he wouldn't release it.

'Please, I——-' He stopped, glancing down at her hand. 'It gets awfully monotonous being confined in this room hour after hour. Most of my friends are guys at the track, and they're pulling out for other races.'

'I'm sorry. I——-' Susan frowned, wondering if it was loneliness she saw flicker across his face, so handsome and proud.

'I don't expect you to make a special trip to see me.' Mitch smiled ruefully, his thumb caressing the inside of her wrist in what appeared an unconscious motion. 'But if you have to come to the hospital to bring Warren's father any more papers, would you come in and say hello?'

The blue eyes held her mesmerized. 'I … I suppose I could,' she surrendered to their spell.

'Thank you.' He carried her fingertips to the soft firmness of his lips, making them tingle from the intimacy of the caress.

There was a rustle of a starched uniform behind Susan, followed by a brisk female voice. 'It's that time again, Mr. Braden.'

Susan pulled her hand free from Mitch's hold, hiding it guiltily behind her back as she spun toward the nurse she had met in the hallway.

'Madge, you have a rotten sense of timing,' Mitch sighed with a mock grimace at her interruption.

The nurse winked broadly at Susan before answering. 'We nurses pride ourselves on being a nuisance.'

'I'd better be going.' Susan quickly gathered up her briefcase as the nurse determinedly held out a thermometer.

'You won't forget to come again?' Mitch held her wavering gaze.

'No,' she admitted in a low voice, wishing she hadn't agreed as she hurried from his room.

There was too much of a risk that word might somehow filter to Robert Sullivan and from there to his son that Susan had seen Mitch Braden, for her to attempt to conceal the visit from Warren. His lips thinned with displeasure at the news, when she told him at dinner that evening.

'Did you really think it was necessary to see him?' he asked churlishly.

'It wasn't necessary,' Susan admitted, studying the rounded chunks of ice in her water goblet rather than meet his censorious dark gaze. 'But since I was right there, it seemed a bit unfeeling not to look in and wish him a speedy recovery.'

'Perhaps,' Warren submitted grudgingly, 'but considering that man's absence of manners, I would hardly worry about doing the polite thing.'

'His behavior is not my concern, nor any reason to behave the same way,' she explained patiently. 'After all, the man has no family here and his friends are mainly people from the race track. If they haven't gone already, they'll be leaving town in the next day or two. It's lonely, confined to a hospital room without any visitors.'

'Braden, lonely?' The disbelieving words were followed by a short, contemptuous laugh. 'I'm certain he has any number of female visitors flocking to his bedside without my fiancée among them!'

'I did not rush to his bedside!' Her nerve ends frayed at the edges. 'I think it's insulting of you to insinuate that I did!'

'I didn't mean to imply that you deliberately did, but I have little doubt that Braden and others would look at it in that light,' Warren retorted. 'Considering the way he's flirted with you so boldly in the past, I'm certain he sees your visit as a sign of encouragement to continue.'

'I did not encourage him,' Susan responded tautly.

Yet, remembering the light kiss on her fingertips, she wondered if unconsciously she had. And she had foolishly said she would see him again.

51

'Not intentionally, but as conceited as he is, he will believe that you did. That's what I've been trying to explain,' he said with impatience.

'All right, you've explained, so let's stop arguing about this.'

'I'm not arguing.' His imposing, masculine features darkened in controlled anger. 'I'm simply forbidding you to see him again.'

Her eyes widened in astonishment, their soft brown color flaming into a snapping fire of temper. Her strong sense of independence asserted itself with a rush as Warren pushed her too far. Being willing to please the man she loved and was going to marry was entirely different from being ruled by him.

'Forbid me! Of all the arrogant———' Susan closed her mouth abruptly, choking on the anger erupting from inside. Uncaring of the possibly interested looks from the other people in the restaurant, she pushed herself out of her chair. 'You may ask me not to see him again, Warren, but nobody *forbids* me to do anything!'

Without a backward glance, she stalked from the table, disregarding his low-voiced command to return. The girl in the cloakroom had just handed her her coat when a glowering Warren appeared at her side. Susan turned to him, lifting her chin defiantly.

'Are you going to take me home, or shall I ask for a taxi?' she challenged.

'What do you think you're doing, making a scene like this?' Warren muttered angrily.

Susan pivoted away. 'I'll get a taxi.'

Her elbow was seized in a rough grip and she was propelled toward the outer door. His hold didn't lessen as he nearly forced her to his car in tight-lipped silence. The crackling tension remained through the entire journey to her home with neither of them uttering a sound.

When the car stopped in front of the house, Susan reached for the door handle. 'I—I believe I owe you an apology, Susan.' Warren seemed to have difficulty in getting the words out.

'I believe you do,' she answered coolly, turning slightly to give him a measuring look.

His hands tightened on the steering wheel as a muscle twitched in his jaw. 'All right, dammit, I'm sorry,' he snapped.

In spite of a faint irritation at his reluctantly offered apology, Susan smiled. The dimness of the car concealed it from Warren.

'And I'm sorry for walking out like that,' she said gently, meeting him halfway.

'The whole argument was silly,' he murmured, taking her into his arms and crushing her tightly against his chest.

'It hurt that you didn't trust me,' she whispered.

In answer, Warren kissed her long and hard as if to drive away the memory of their angry words. Susan responded with equal intensity to show him that all was forgiven, if not totally forgotten. Afterwards she lay curled contentedly in the hollow of his shoulder while his hand absently massaged the soft flesh of her arm.

'Please, darling,' Warren said in a low, husky voice, 'I'm asking you not to see that man any more.'

Tensing slightly, Susan had the uncomfortable feeling that his apology and the subsequent kiss had been designed to lull her into the sense of security she was now enjoying. The end result would be that he would achieve the very thing he had set out to.

A tiny frown of uncertainty touched her forehead. 'I—I'm sorry, Warren, but I can't give you an answer. I simply won't promise that I might not see him again,' she murmured, darting a cautious glance into his passive, rugged features.

For an instant his expression seemed to harden and Susan thought the argument was going to begin all over again. Then he relaxed his mouth into a dry smile.

'The fact that you love me is the only answer I need, I guess,' he said softly.

A sigh of gratitude slid from her lips as she mentally chided herself for thinking such mean thoughts against his motives. She had hated accusing him of trying to use underhanded methods to extract a promise from her.

'Thank you, darling,' she whispered.

He placed a quick kiss on her lips. 'Come on,' he said, dislodging her from her comfortable nest in his arm. 'It's time you were going in the house. You have to be at work in the morning and you know what a tyrant your boss can be.'

'He's a regular monster,' Susan laughed as she moved to her own side of the car. Opening the car door, she glanced over her shoulder at his smiling face. 'Goodnight, darling."

'Goodnight,' Warren responded, his voice a gentle caress.

The next day the necessity arose again for Susan to transport some important documents to Robert Sullivan at the hospital. The words were there in Warren's eyes, asking her again not to see Mitch Braden while she was there. Susan looked away, unable to give him the answer he wanted.

All night and for the better part of the day she had been trying to come to a decision. As she walked down the hospital corridor to Robert Sullivan's room, she knew she had reached it.

After she had given the papers to Warren's father, she would see Mitch. She would see Mitch and tactfully tell him that it would be better for all concerned if she didn't see him any more. After telling Mitch she would look in, she would look in; she simply could not do it without explaining why.

Keeping her gaze averted from the door to Mitch's room, Susan intended to walk straight by. First she wanted to see Robert Sullivan, then she would go to Mitch.

'Susan!' Mitch's delighted voice interrupted her plan.

She paused, glancing over her shoulder to see him standing in the doorway. He looked disturbingly attractive in a knee-length robe of camel brown, one sleeve empty and the bulge of the cast beneath the tied front.

'Hello, Mitch.' She swallowed and curved her mouth into a taut smile. 'I was on my way to Mr. Sullivan's room with some more papers. I—I was going to stop in to see you on my way out.'

'I somehow didn't think there would be any errand that would bring you back today,' he smiled slowly.

'It came up suddenly.'

'I'm glad.'

'Yes … well.' Susan breathed in deeply, bowing her head to break away from the blue glitter of his eyes.

'Would it upset everything if you came here before going to his room?' Mitch asked, gesturing down the hallway with his right hand.

Susan hesitated indecisively. 'No, no, I don't suppose it would.'

But she walked very slowly toward Mitch, not quite knowing what she was going to say to him now that the moment had arrived sooner than she had anticipated. He stepped aside to let her pass, meeting her nervous sideways glance with a faint dimpling smile.

A few steps inside the room, she stopped short, meeting the curious and speculating gaze of the brawny man sprawled in the chair beside the bed.

'Excuse me,' she stammered, turning quickly to Mitch. 'You should have said you already had a visitor. I'll come back later.'

Mitch blocked her path to the door with casual ease. 'Stay,' he insisted. 'Mike was just leaving, weren't you, Mike?' Mitch glanced pointedly at the man with the thinning dark hair.

The man's mouth turned up at the corners, smiling at some secret thing as he pushed himself out of the chair. 'That's right. I was just leaving.' He didn't leave, but stood there expectantly waiting for an introduction.

'You needn't go on my account,' Susan said quickly.

'Honestly, miss, I was about to leave before you came,' the man assured her in an amused voice. Still he waited.

Out of the corner of her eye, Susan saw Mitch shake his head in resignment. 'Susan, this hairy-chested Irishman is Mike O'Brian, my pit boss and sometimes my friend. This is Susan Mabry, Mike.'

'I'm pleased to meet you, Mr. O'Brian.' Her hand was lost in the hugeness of his.

54

'Mike,' he corrected her formality with a friendly smile. 'I recognized you, Susan.' At her blank look, he added, 'From the restaurant.'

Her cheeks warmed as she realized he must have been one of the men who had joined Mitch the first time she saw him. A swift glance at Mitch caught the narrowing look he gave Mike, warning him into silence.

Mike released her hand. 'It was nice meeting you.' Then he turned to Mitch. 'We'll be pulling out in the morning, so take care.'

'I will,' Mitch nodded affirmatively. 'Don't enjoy your vacation too much. I shouldn't be in this cast very long.'

'You wait until the doctor tells you to take it off or I'll break it again for you!' Mike smiled his threat.

There was a brief clasp of hands between the two, then Mike left the room. Susan felt Mitch's gaze on her and moved toward the window.

'You're looking much better today,' she said to fill the silence.

'The dizziness seems to have gone, so the doctors let me up,' he replied. 'Now that you're here, I'm feeling much better.'

Susan fingered the leather case in her hands. 'Don't say things like that, Mitch.'

'What did I say?' His voice held false innocence.

'It wasn't what you said but what you implied,' she answered, pressing her lips together tightly.

He walked slowly toward her. She could hear his footsteps bringing him nearer, but refused to turn around.

'And you don't like it when I imply that I find the sight of you stimulating to the senses,' Mitch stated.

'No, I don't.' Susan stared at the whiteness of her fingers clenching the case handle. 'You can't keep ignoring the fact that I'm engaged.'

'I don't ignore it, exactly,' he corrected with faint amusement. 'But, since you don't like me to tell you how very beautiful you are, we'll talk of other things. Greg came to see me last night and your father looked in this morning while he was doing his hospital rounds.'

Susan sighed, a crazy kind of misery welling up inside. She turned from the window, meeting his level gaze. She wished for the calm possession displayed in his handsome face.

'This isn't going to work either,' she protested lamely. 'I can't make small talk. I was going to come here today because there was something I wanted to tell you.'

His gaze moved to the top of her head. 'Do you know when the light hits your hair just right it has a fiery glint, crimson red like flames? Yet your hair is such a very dark shade of brown.'

'Don't try to change the subject, Mitch. I'm serious.'

'So am I,' he agreed. 'In certain lights, your hair is definitely red.'

'I don't want to discuss the color of my hair. That's not why I came.' Frustrated, Susan turned back to the window.

'I know why you came,' Mitch said quietly. 'You came to tell me you aren't going to visit me any more.'

Her head jerked toward him in surprise. 'How did you know?'

'Call it a calculated guess,' he shrugged indifferently, and stared out the window. 'What happened? Did your jealous fiancé find out that you'd seen me and forbid you to come?'

'He didn't forbid me.' She wasn't about to tell him that Warren had tried. 'And he didn't find out, I told him.'

'You told him and he didn't forbid you to see me? I find that hard to believe.' He grinned crookedly at her, his bronze features glowing attractively in the sunlight.

'I never said he liked the idea,' Susan protested as her pulse quickened under his glittering look. 'He doesn't altogether understand why I'm seeing you.'

'Do you?' Mitch taunted softly.

'Yes,' she looked quickly away. 'It's never any fun being in a hospital, and not having any visitors makes it even worse. I—I was trying to be kind and compassionate.'

'I see,' he drawled with an undertone of amusement. 'Now you've decided that to keep peace with your fiancé, it's best not to see me any more.'

'That's what I decided,' Susan agreed, unconsciously touching the diamond solitaire on her finger. 'I have to be fair with Warren.'

'I'm afraid you have a problem.'

'What?' She slid a wary sideways glance at his face.

Mitch continued to gaze complacently out the window. 'The doctor will be releasing me from the hospital tomorrow morning or Friday at the very latest.'

'And?' Susan frowned, not seeing how that news would present her with any difficulty.

'And,' there was a wicked light in the blue eyes when he looked at her, 'your father has invited me to dinner on Friday night.'

'No,' she denied in a small voice.

'Yes,' Mitch nodded firmly.

'But you can't go!' she protested.

'I have already accepted the invitation.'

'You can phone Dad and tell him you can't come,' Susan insisted. 'You can think of some excuse to refuse.'

'But I'm not going to refuse,' Mitch said patiently.

'You must.'

'Why? I like your family and I'm looking forward to one of your mother's home-cooked meals. I don't see any reason I should deny myself the pleasure simply because you have a jealous fiancé. He's going to have to learn to trust you more.'

'Warren trusts me,' Susan defended.

Mitch chuckled softly. 'Of course, it's me that he doesn't trust, and with good reason. He knows I want you.'

'Stop saying things like that!' She spun away from him, angry at him for not refusing the invitation and for the daring and disturbing statement he had just made. 'I'm engaged to Warren!'

'You are beginning to sound like a broken record,' he taunted.

'I'll repeat myself a thousand times if that's how many it takes before you accept what I'm saying!' Her eyes flashed angrily at his mocking expression.

Sobering, Mitch studied her intently for several long seconds, gazing so deeply into her eyes that she had the uncanny sensation that he knew what she was thinking. Then, slowly, his firm male mouth grooved into a smile, carving faint dimples into the smooth, lean cheeks.

'You only have nine hundred-odd times to go,' he told her.

'Oh!' Her foot stamped the floor in a childish tantrum. 'It's hopeless trying to reason with you! Warren said you were much too conceited, and he was right!'

'Do you mean Warren *isn't* always right? Her outburst only deepened his mocking smile.

Blinking back the furious tears of rage that scalded her eyes, Susan stalked from the room.

'I'll see you on Friday night.' Mitch's parting jibe was followed by a throaty chuckle that whipped her already raw nerves. If she had looked back she might have gained some satisfaction from seeing his immediate grimace of pain because of his cracked ribs.

Almost an hour later, she tapped on the connecting door to Warren's office, waiting for his summons before entering. He glanced up from the papers spread before him, straightening against the tall-backed leather chair as he recognized her.

'Did you get the papers safely delivered to my father?' But his dark, inspecting eyes asked an entirely different question.

'Yes, I did.' Susan walked to his desk and handed him the keys to his car.

'Good,' Warren nodded, and paused expectantly.

Susan's arms were stiffly held to her sides. She knew she could avoid answering his unasked question. She also knew she could avoid mentioning Mitch's intention to join her family for dinner on Friday evening. Unfortunately there was an excellent chance that her family, especially her brother, might not be so silent about it.

'I saw Mitch today.' Susan tried to make it sound like an unexpected happening that was of little importance. Warren said nothing and waited. 'I told him I wouldn't be visiting him any more.'

'Susan!' Warren breathed warmly. He leaned forward in his chair, a smile lightening his imposing and rugged features.

'Wait.' She held up a cautioning hand. 'There's something else I have to tell you.'

His dark head tipped to the side in wariness. 'What?'

'My father has invited Mitch Braden to dinner on Friday night and he has accepted.'

'Your father! Good God!' Warren breathed in deeply, a black mask stealing again over his face. 'Why?'

'How should I know why?' Susan shrugged with bewildered anger. 'I suppose it was a combination of reasons. My family have already met him. My father is a racing fan and I guess he got along rather well with Mitch the last time. Greg practically hero-worships him as you know. Mother agreed, probably because she felt sorry for him, because of the accident and all. In any case, he's coming to dinner and there isn't anything I can do about it.'

'I wouldn't be surprised to learn that he did everything but ask to be invited,' Warren muttered 'And I'm tied up Friday night. I wonder if he knew about that, too.'

'Really, Warren, he isn't omniscient,' she chided.

'Sometimes I wonder about that Indy man.' He shook his head. 'I just don't like the idea of you being alone with him for an entire evening.'

'With Greg and Amy and Mom and Dad, I'm hardly going to be alone with him,' she pointed out.

'You know what I mean.'

'Yes,' Susan agreed, knowing that in some way Mitch would make his presence felt. 'If I thought I wouldn't have to do a lot of tall explaining to Dad, I would arrange to be out. Besides, I don't want it to look as if I'm running away from him.'

'You're right,' he conceded. 'You might as well plan to be home. He might as well see that you belong to me even when I'm not around.'

6

ore coffee, Mitch?' her mother offered as he sat back in his chair.
'Nothing more, thanks, Beth,' he replied, shaking his head
and raising his hand in refusal. 'My ribs are already saying I've
eaten too much.'
Susan's teeth grated against each other. Less than half an hour after Greg
had brought him from his hotel, Mitch had been calling her parents by their
Christian names. The easy friendliness between them irritated her.

'More remembered last time that you said Swiss steak was your favorite,
so she fixed it especially for you tonight,' Amy said. 'And I helped.'

'I guess I have to divide my compliments to the chef between the two of
you,' Mitch smiled. 'I'm flattered that you remembered, Beth.'

'Thank you.' Her mother was momentarily flustered and Susan
seethed inwardly.

'There's nothing that can replace a home-cooked meal,' her father stated.

'I'd forgotten what I'd been missing,' Mitch agreed ruefully.

'Yeah, but you lead such an exciting life.' Greg glanced at him enviously.
'Mom's a great cook, but———' He shrugged his shoulders to indicate that
food was not important compared to the adventures Mitch had known.

'I thought the same way when I was your age, Greg.' The mockingly raised brow held gentle understanding. 'But ten years of living in hotels and eating in restaurants can make a man reevaluate his thinking. Hotel rooms can be very sterile and lonely when you have to walk into them night after night.'

'Haven't you ever considered settling down?' Beth Mabry asked with maternal concern.

Through the veil of his spiky dark lashes, his blue eyes glittered at Susan. She met the look with determined indifference.

'Until recently, I was much too busy.' His gaze swung back to her mother. 'A time or two I've considered buying a house or renting an apartment so I could say I had a home base. But without someone to share it with, it would have been no different from a hotel room.'

'You're a very attractive man. I find it hard to believe you haven't found anyone you were willing to share a home with,' Beth Mabry laughed with gentle disbelief.

'You have to realize I'm seldom in one place long enough to really get acquainted with anyone. And the chances of meeting someone—say, like your daughter——-' Mitch looked at Susan again, but she kept her eyes downcast, knowing they were flashing with temper again, 'is unlikely in my profession.'

'And when you do, the girl is probably engaged, like myself,' Susan couldn't resist inserting in sugared tones.

'Exactly,' Mitch agreed.

'I still think it would be an exciting life,' Greg insisted. 'When I get older, that's what I want to do.'

'If you live that long,' Simon Mabry said dryly.

'You used to drive race cars, Dad. I'm just taking after you,' Susan's brother pointed out with a sly grin.

Mitch glanced to her father, his head cocked inquiringly on one side. 'You didn't mention that, Simon.'

'It was years ago, when I was in college,' he shrugged. 'At the time it seemed like an easy way to pick up some extra money. When you're young and foolish, you do a lot of things without thinking about the risks.'

'Why did you quit, Dad?' Amy forgot her young lady act and curled her feet beneath her on the straight-backed chair. 'You could have become a famous racer like Mitch.'

'Two reasons, actually,' he smiled and glanced at his wife, sitting at the opposite end of the table from him. 'The first being the fact that I met your mother. For a while, even after we were married, I rather enjoyed the image of being the dashing adventurer until she told me one night that Susan was on the way. That rather woke me up to the responsibilities I owed to my

60

future family. I had planned to continue racing until Susan was born so I could have the extra money to pay the doctor and hospital bills. Then one day I was working on my car—I couldn't afford to share my small winnings with a mechanic—and the wrench slipped. I broke all the fingers on my left hand. At that point, I realized that what I really wanted to be was a doctor and I was terrified that the injury to my hand might have finished that dream for good. It didn't. The very next day after the accident, I sold the car.'

'When you get married, Mitch, will you give up racing?' Amy propped an elbow on her knee and rested her chin in her hand.

'No, I don't think so,' he mused absently. 'Eventually I'll have to, of course. Unlike your father, I want to race cars. It's my life.'

'Isn't that being slightly arrogant?' Susan said tightly. 'What you would be telling the woman you married is that this is your life and she can take it or leave it. Surely she has some say in your joint future?'

A steel blue gaze focused on her, his expression unyielding yet not cold or angry. 'I'm willing to take her as she is and not attempt to change her. Is it wrong to expect the same in return? Or even arrogant?'

Susan looked away from the unwavering directness of his gaze. Her small bubble of indignation was pricked by his reasonable request.

'I suppose not,' she admitted with quiet reluctance.

'It would be rather like asking Warren to give up his law practice, wouldn't it?' her mother put in rhetorically. 'A woman would learn to adjust to the dangers of your job in the same way that I've accepted the life of a doctor. I never thought of it like that before, but it's true.'

'I don't see what all the fuss is about,' Amy declared airily, uncurling her legs and rising from the chair. She tossed her head, sending her long hair dancing about her shoulders and catching fire from the overhead light. 'I think it would be super to be married to a race car driver.'

Greg laughed. 'Everything with you is "super." The dinner was "super." The movie was "super,"' he mimicked.

'Oh, what do you know about it?' Amy accused, her temper flaring that her brother should make fun of her in front of Mitch.

Beth Mabry rose to her feet. 'I think it's about time we made washing the dishes "super."'

'Come on, Mitch,' her father grinned. 'That's a signal for us to leave the room before she ties an apron around our waists.'

'It was a delicious meal, Beth,' Mitch offered, wincing slightly at the pain in his rib cage when he rose from the chair. Then he winked at Amy. 'Prepared by a pair of "super" cooks.'

Amy giggled and quickly covered her mouth with a hand as if wishing she had made a more adult reaction. Susan's mouth tightened grimly as she quickly began stacking the dishes on the table rather than watch her father and Mitch leave the dining room.

Her younger sister was dreamily watching him go. He seemed to have her entire family in the palm of his hand, Susan thought disgustedly.

'Amy, would you stop mooning over that man and help clear the table!' Susan snapped.

'I am not mooning over him!' Amy's eyes widened indignantly. 'And you don't have to be so grouchy!'

Sinking her teeth into her lower lip, Susan bit back an even sharper retort, knowing it wasn't fair to take her temper out on Amy. Her sister was at an impressionable age where her crushes were painfully deep and short-lived.

'Besides,' Amy lifted her chin to a haughty angle, 'it's my turn to wipe the dishes and it's your job to clear the table,' she declared before flouncing into the kitchen.

Susan glanced at her mother and sighed. 'Was I ever that hopeless?'

'We all were,' her mother smiled faintly, and picked up a stack of dishes, carrying them into the kitchen.

Susan followed within minutes carrying more dishes. She opened the door in time to hear Amy ask, 'How long will Mitch be staying tonight, Mom?'

'I don't know. I imagine until your father drives him to his hotel. Why?' Beth Mabry replied, adjusting the temperature of the water coming out of the double sink taps.

'Couldn't I wipe the dishes after he leaves?' Amy pleaded. 'I mean, he's just got out of the hospital and all. He might be tired and ask to leave early.'

'I'm sure he'll stay until after the dishes are done,' her mother answered with a straight face but a decided twinkle in her eyes that met Susan's raised eyebrows of despair.

'We could leave the dishes altogether,' Amy suggested, unwilling to give up with one refusal. 'I promise I'll help you do them in the morning.'

'The answer is "no," Amy.'

'If you would help, Amy,' Susan put in with thinning patience, 'instead of standing around trying to think of reasons not to do the dishes, we might finish them sooner. Besides, I'm certain Mitch Braden can survive without your company for a little while.'

Amy whirled about. 'Just because you don't like him, Susan, it's no reason why I can't! And don't be telling me what I should do!'

'Susan,' her mother said with astonishment, 'don't you like Mitch?'

'Of course I like him,' Susan answered nervously, 'but I certainly don't think he's some Greek god who's come down from Olympus to walk with us mortals the way Amy does. He's just a man.'

'But what a man!' Amy retorted smugly. 'Compared to him, Warren is a stiff-necked prude.'

'Mother,' Susan breathed in deeply, 'if you don't do something about this daughter of yours, so help me, I will!'

'Stop it, both of you!' was the stern response.

Returning to the dining room, Susan finished clearing the table. She had resolved not to lose her temper with Amy, then lost it anyway. She herself had felt the force of Mitch's attraction. Amy was so young and vulnerable that it was only natural she should fall under his spell.

With the dining room straightened and all the chairs in the proper place at the table, Susan walked back into the kitchen straight to her young sister.

'I'll finish drying the dishes for you,' she said, taking the towel from Amy's hands. 'Go on into the living room.' She smiled at the joy gleaming instantaneously in her sister's face. 'And I'm sorry for putting you down.'

'Oh, Susan, you are super!' Amy hugged her quickly and dashed from the room. Susan could hear her footsteps slow to a more ladylike pace before she reached the living room.

The dishes were finished in short order and Susan was compelled by a sense of polite duty to follow her mother into the living room. She chose a chair apart from the others, curling up in a shadowed corner which allowed her an unobstructed view of her family and Mitch Braden.

Despite the armless sleeve and the bulging cast beneath his shirt, he looked leanly powerful, like the coiled muscular shape of a jungle cat. The lampshade kept the light from touching off the golden fire of his brown hair, but a blue light seemed to glow warmly in his eyes.

Her family was so at ease with him. The conversation wasn't stilted as it often was when Warren visited them. She had expected Mitch to dominate the discussion, but he had a knack of drawing others into the conversation.

Except herself, that was. He seemed to sense her faint hostility. She guessed he had been aware of it all evening and was now leaving her alone. Fine, she told herself, that was what she wanted, but she felt strangely left out, and it didn't help to remind herself that it was her own choice.

The cuckoo clock sang out the ten o'clock hour. Mitch glanced at his wristwatch as if to confirm the time.

'I'm sorry, I didn't realize it was so late,' he apologized warmly. 'I hadn't intended to outstay my welcome.'

'You aren't leaving already?' Amy moaned.

'It's late, Red,' Mitch smiled, then glanced to her father. 'There isn't any need for you to go out again tonight. I'll call a cab.'

'Nonsense,' Simon Mabry refused vigorously. 'The night air will do me good. I won't hear of you taking a cab.'

'I appreciate your kindness,' Mitch said with a nod of submission. 'I can't thank you enough for this evening. You've all made me feel very welcome.'

'I wish you didn't have to leave,' said Greg with obvious sincerity.

'So do I,' Mitch agreed as he carefully rose to his feet. 'My hotel room is going to seem awfully cold and silent after an evening in your home, Beth. Thank you.'

'Why do you have to go back there?' Amy frowned, a faint pout on her lips. 'I don't see why you couldn't stay here with us.'

'Then I definitely would wear out my welcome.' The lines around his mouth deepened with a gentle smile.

Susan breathed a silent sigh of relief at his instant refusal. For a second, she had thought he was going to make some wistful remark.

'That's an idea,' her father said thoughtfully and Susan's eyes widened in apprehension. 'We do have that guest room upstairs, Beth. Nobody uses it for anything.'

'Simon——'Mitch held up his hand.

'He's right,' Beth Mabry interrupted. 'We would be happy to have you stay with us, Mitch.'

'I couldn't take advantage of your generosity that way,' he shook his head in refusal.

'You wouldn't be taking advantage of us,' Beth insisted. 'If we didn't want you to stay, we wouldn't have asked. And one more person in this house isn't going to be any extra trouble. The way Greg and Amy are always inviting their friends over I've become used to it.'

'It's a tempting invitation, Beth, but I don't think I should accept it,' Mitch refused again.

Susan, who had been staring in open-mouthed protest, finally spoke out. 'We understand, Mitch. We wouldn't want you to do anything you would regret. After all, you're used to coming and going as you please and you would probably feel your movements were restricted, staying here with us.'

His level blue gaze focused on her and a sudden merry twinkle came into his eyes. 'On the contrary, Susan,' he smiled, 'I was more concerned that your parents might regret inviting a stranger into their home.'

'You're not a stranger!' Amy denied vehemently.

'In truth I must agree,' Simon Mabry added. 'Speaking for myself, I feel as if we've known you for a very long time. We would be happy to have you if you would like to stay.'

'Well, if you insist on twisting my arm,' Mitch shrugged, smiling crookedly, 'I guess I have no choice but to accept.'

Amy cheered unabashedly while Susan trembled with impotent rage. How could she possibly live under the same roof with him for the three or four weeks he would be staying?

64

She was filled with the uneasy premonition that nothing would be the same after he left. Her life would be irrevocably altered.

Greg scrambled to his feet. 'I'll come along with Dad and help you pack up your things at the hotel. You can move in tonight. Wow! Wait until the fellers hear about this!' his voice cracked in excitement.

'No, it's too late tonight,' Mitch stated. 'I'll have everything packed and ready to go tomorrow at noon. That will give you time to reconsider the invitation. And I promise I'll understand if you change your mind.'

'We won't,' Amy declared as if making a solemn vow.

Unmindful of the startled looks she received from her family, Susan muttered a hurried 'Excuse me' and walked quickly from the room. She had no particular destination in mind. She wasn't even conscious of where she was when she came to a stop in front of the kitchen sink.

Yanking open a cupboard door above her head, she removed a drinking glass and filled it with cold water from the tap. She was just lifting it to her lips when the kitchen door opened. She counted to ten before turning toward it, expecting to see the reproving face of her mother.

'Do you always sulk when things don't go the way you want?' Mitch asked in a low voice laced with curious amusement.

'How could you do this?' Susan hissed angrily.

'Do what?' he repeated with deliberate blankness. 'All I've done is accept a neighborly invitation,' he drawled lazily.

'Yes,' she was so angry she could hardly speak, 'all you did was accept an invitation you did everything but get on your knees and ask for!'

'Are you implying that I tricked your parents into inviting me to stay here?' His hurt, affronted look might have seemed genuine if it wasn't for the sparkle in his eyes.

'Yes,' she snapped.

'You really believe I could be that devious?'

'Yes!'

A brow raised briefly in resignation. 'Time is running out on me. I have to take advantage of every minute that I can.'

'What does that mean?' Susan demanded guardedly.

'You're a smart girl, I think you'll figure it out,' he smiled. 'Good night, Beautiful. I'll see you tomorrow.'

He was being deliberately mysterious to confuse her and sidetrack her from the issue. Her fingers tightened around the glass of water in her hand, then paused.

'I wouldn't throw that glass if I were you,' he warned in a silently laughing tone. 'I think you'd have difficulty explaining to your parents how dropping a glass splattered water all over the walls and door.'

The second time the door opened, it was Beth Mabry who entered. Susan raised the glass to her mouth and took a long gulp of water.

'What's the matter?' her mother asked quietly.

'It's just going to be awful.' Susan avoided the gentle gaze studying her.

'What is?'

'Mitch Braden living here, that's what.' She set the partially empty glass on the counter with an impatient movement of her hand.

'Now, why do you say that?' Her mother's curiosity was overridden with surprise as she walked to the counter where Susan stood.

'Because——-' Susan glanced up, her expression stretched taut to control the desperate anger that wanted to erupt. 'Because Warren is jealous.'

'Jealous? Of Mitch Braden? For heaven's sake, why?'

This time Susan related the exact circumstances surrounding her first meeting with Mitch Braden and the subsequent encounters, not omitting the way Mitch constantly flirted with her.

'Does Warren know all of this?' Beth asked when Susan had finished. Her expression was gentle with understanding, but there was a faint gleam of amusement in her eyes that Susan found irritating.

'Of course he doesn't know all of it. He would be positively furious if he knew everything. But I swear, Mother, he isn't going to understand why you've invited Mitch to stay here. For that matter, neither do I.'

'Yes, you do,' her mother smiled. 'Perhaps if I'd known about the way things were between Mitch and Warren I might have considered the invitation more thoroughly before inviting him to stay here. But we certainly can't retract it now even if we wanted to, not unless you want to explain this whole story to the others.'

'Greg would have a field day with it,' Susan sighed, running a weary hand through the dark hair near her ear.

'Besides, you and Warren are engaged. And since you've done nothing to encourage Mitch,' there was a faint pause as Susan suddenly averted her head, 'then I think Warren should learn to trust you and to accept that you can handle the situation. Mitch isn't staying for ever, just a few weeks.'

'It's going to seem like an eternity,' Susan sighed.

'You're beginning to exaggerate like your younger sister,' her mother teased dryly.

Smiling ruefully, Susan pushed herself away from the counter. 'If it wasn't so painful being thirteen, then I'd wish I was Amy's age. Goodnight Mom.'

'It will all work out for the best, Susan.'

'Sure,' she answered in a doubting-Thomas voice.

Early on Saturday afternoon, Mitch moved in bag and baggage. The house was in a gleeful turmoil the entire afternoon. Mr. Mabry had decided the garage had to be cleaned out to make room for Mitch's sports car. He had driven it over for him since Mitch couldn't manage the gearshifts with his broken arm.

Susan tried to stay out of the mainstream as much as she could, but the excitement rippling through the house touched her in spite of her attempts to remain outside its sphere.

Each time she caught herself about to join the laughter and chatting voices of her family and Mitch, she would remind herself of Warren's reaction when he came to pick her up for their date that night.

It was difficult being miserable when everyone else was having fun.

As Susan dressed for her date with Warren, she considered Mitch's attitude toward her that day. He had seemed to pay little attention to her. She had expected him to be smugly triumphant, ready to remind her mockingly of his presence in her home at every opportunity. Yet he had been as friendly with her as he had been with the rest of the family.

It wouldn't last, she sighed into the bathroom mirror. He was merely biding his time. She couldn't afford to relax her guard even for an instant.

The sound of a car pulling into the drive drifted through the screened windows, opened to admit the warm breeze of the early summer's night. Adding the finishing stroke of lipstick, Susan hurried to her room, picking up the crocheted shawl from her bed before hurrying out again for the staircase. Warren was early.

The doorbell rang when she reached the top of the stairs. Before her toe touched the first step, a voice called out from the living room below.

'I'll answer it!' Mitch stated.

Susan's heart nose-dived to her shoes. Her legs were paralyzed, unable to carry her down the flight of steps before Mitch reached the front door.

Whistling absently, he appeared below her, the empty white shirt-sleeve tucked into the waistband of his trousers.

The door was swung open and Susan could just barely see the dark gray of Warren's trousers. She could visualize the stunned look on his face.

'Hello, Warren. Come on in,' Mitch greeted, inviting him in as if he had done it a thousand times before, just as if he was a permanent member of the household.

He stepped to one side to allow Warren entry, brown head turning toward the stairs where Susan waited in dread.

'Susan, it's for you!' Mitch called loudly, then paused as he met her gaze. 'Sorry, I didn't see you standing there.'

'I just bet you didn't,' Susan thought savagely when she saw the wicked glint in the blue eyes. She averted her gaze to the steps before her as the paralysis left her legs and she started down.

67

'Warren is here to pick you up,' Mitch announced unnecessarily.

'I can see that,' Susan snapped tightly.

One look at the glowering mask of rage on Warren's face told her in no uncertain terms what he thought of the freehanded way Mitch was making himself at home. Susan hurried her pace, fearing an explosion at any second.

With infuriating calm, Mitch waited at the bottom of the stairs with Warren, his mocking gaze watching her descent and knowing the reason for the flush of anger in her cheeks.

Deliberately she ignored Mitch to look directly at Warren. 'I'm ready if you are,' she said, reaching out for Warren's arm.

'You two have a nice time,' Mitch offered as Warren pivoted sharply around to leave. 'Don't keep Susan out too late. She needs her beauty sleep.' There was mocking emphasis on beauty before he closed the door behind them.

Warren began striding toward his car, indifferent to the fact that Susan had to practically run to keep up with him. 'Would you kindly explain to me what he's doing there?' His voice vibrated with checked rage.

'You aren't going to like it,' Susan said in a very hesitant voice.

He held the car door open for her, his dark gaze sweeping her apprehensive face, its coldness chilling her to the bone.

'There's nothing about the man that I like, and I have the feeling I'll like this even less.'

Susan waited until he was in the car before dropping her bombshell. The response was what she expected and dreaded.

'You can't be serious! You can't possibly mean he's going to be living in the same house with you!'

'I'm perfectly serious,' she replied in a forced calm voice.

'Your parents actually invited him to stay!' Warren shook his head in disbelief. 'Didn't you tell them what kind of man he is?'

'What could I tell them?' Susan reasoned. 'That he pays me outrageous compliments? That he flirts with me? They would have laughed and asked him anyway. They like him.'

'So you're just accepting it?' he accused grimly. 'You're not making any attempt to change the situation?'

'What would you have me do, Warren?' The impatience she felt toward the whole mess she was in and Warren's lack of understanding about her helplessness to correct it made her voice sharp. 'Move out?'

'You could at least consider it,' he snapped.

'He isn't going to live there permanently, only for a few weeks,' she reminded him.

'I have a feeling there's going to be trouble,' Warren muttered.

Susan echoed the thought, but only to herself.

7

usan walked into the kitchen. 'Is there anything I can help you with, Mom, before Warren comes?'

Glancing up from the salad bowl in front of her, Beth Mabry cut the last tomato into wedges and let them join the others in the red mound on top of the lettuce. She surveyed her daughter quickly, taking in the freshness of the yellow sun-dress with its varying sized circles of white polka dots.

'Yes, you can toss this salad together while I scrub some potatoes to bake,' she answered, drying her hands on a terry dish towel. As Susan moved toward her, Beth paused. 'On second thought, you'd better have Greg take the charcoal out and get the barbecue grill started. I think he's in the garage tinkering with his car.'

'I'll finish the salad when I come back, then,' Susan nodded, and walked toward the kitchen door that led directly into the garage.

As she opened the door, she heard Mitch say, 'Try it again, Greg.'

Her brother was partially sitting behind the wheel of his car, the door open, and Mitch was bending to look under the hood. Greg turned the key in the ignition. There was a whining growl and nothing happened. With an impatient grimace, Greg stepped out and walked to the front of the car where Mitch was intently studying the motor.

'Greg, Mom wants you to take the charcoal out back and get the grill started,' Susan told him, her gaze unwillingly drawn to Mitch, who didn't even look up at the sound of her voice.

He was wearing a pair of soiled overalls in a deep shade of azure blue, the plaster cast on his arm concealed behind the zippered front.

'Not now, Susan,' Greg muttered with a dismissing glance. 'I'm busy.'

'If you want to eat before dark, you'd better go do it now,' she replied. 'It won't take you that long.'

'You might as well.' Mitch straightened. 'This isn't something we're going to fix in a few minutes.'

And still he didn't look at Susan. Ever since Saturday night he had seemed to take her existence for granted, as if her presence in the house didn't warrant any special attention. Mitch hadn't ignored her, but he had treated her no differently than he had the rest of the family. He could have been her older brother.

'Oh, all right. I'll start the stupid grill,' Greg grumbled, his lanky frame moving with a long stride to a corner of the garage where the bag of charcoal briquets sat. Picking it up, he roughly shoved open the rear door leading into the back yard and kicked it shut with his foot.

Mitch started to fiddle with something under the hood and Susan turned to leave, not really certain why she had waited.

'Would you mind lighting me a cigarette, Susan?' Mitch asked absently. 'My hand is all greasy. The pack is sitting on the work bench. The lighter should be there, too.' He waved in the general direction of the counter built into the rear wall of one side of the garage.

Susan hesitated briefly, then walked to the counter, littered with various kinds of garden and mechanical tools. She took a cigarette from the pack and lit it, surprised to find the hand that held the lighter was trembling slightly. She turned to give it to him as he walked toward her, an absent frown of concentration on his handsome face.

Instead of reaching for the cigarette, his right hand removed a rag from the work bench. His head tipped sideways toward Susan, indicating she should place the lit cigarette in his mouth. She did so reluctantly, but he barely seemed to notice her at all.

'Thanks,' he offered, speaking through the cigarette between his lips. He tried, ineffectively, to wipe the worst of the grime off his hand. Then he sighed. 'How does a man with one hand wash the dirt off that hand?'

'That's a good question,' Susan laughed shortly. The amusement that glittered in his eyes was casually friendly. It was impossible to take offense at his comment when he was directing it against himself. 'I suppose you'll have to have someone else do it for you.'

'I suppose so,' he agreed, squinting his eyes against the smoke before gingerly removing the cigarette from his mouth with two still darkly soiled fingers. He arched his back slightly and winced at the pull the movement exerted on his injured rib cage.

'You really shouldn't be working on that car,' Susan said reprovingly, 'not in your condition.'

'I'm only giving Greg a hand.' Mitch smoothly dismissed the idea that he might be overtaxing himself. 'He's doing all the heavy work.' He leaned against the counter and ran an appraising eye over her dress. 'This is Tuesday night, isn't it? That means you have a date with Warren.'

It was a casual comment without an undertone of mockery. 'That's right,' she admitted cautiously. 'He'll be here to pick me up in a little while.'

'You don't sound very enthusiastic.' He tipped his head to the side, a pose of vague curiosity.

'I—I don't know what you mean.' Her chin lifted slightly as if she sensed a coming need for a defensive attitude.

'The man you're engaged to is going to be here in a little while, and you sound so matter-of-fact about it,' he explained with indifference.

'Well, it is a fact,' Susan shrugged, a faint frown of bewilderment clouding her forehead.

'Aren't you excited about seeing him again?'

'I just saw him when I left the office at five,' she reminded him. 'It isn't as though I haven't seen him for a couple of days.'

'Of course,' Mitch agreed with a wry smile. 'I guess I was letting myself be influenced by a lot of romantic nonsense. I assumed that you would miss him no matter how short the time since the last time you saw him.'

'Naturally I miss him,' Susan retorted, almost too quickly.

'Naturally?' A brown brow arched with arrogant mockery. 'You sound very offhand. Are your dates becoming too routine?'

'What do you expect me to do? Fling myself in his arms every time I see him?'

Mitch smiled. 'I'm not expecting anything. I was only commenting on the fact that you seem to display little emotion where Warren is concerned.'

Her head lifted to a haughty angle. 'I save any emotional display for when we're alone,' she informed him icily.

'Then the two of you do indulge in a little necking?'

'I don't see that it's any of your business.'

'It isn't, not really.' The laughing blue eyes moved to her mouth, thinned into a disapproving line.

'Then you shouldn't have brought it up,' Susan replied with biting arrogance.

'I couldn't help it. You have a very kissable pair of lips, and I didn't like to think of them going to waste,' he mocked.

'I assure you they don't.'

Her heartbeat skipped erratically as he studied the movement of her mouth when she spoke. It was unnerving. Susan could feel a warmth start in her midsection and slowly begin to spread through her veins.

'I wonder if anyone taught Warren to share when he was a little boy,' Mitch mused absently, his gaze not wavering from her mouth.

Her breathing became shallow and restricted. She knew she had to escape and quickly. That indefinable magnetism was reaching out for her.

She averted her face sharply. 'I have to go and help Mom in the kitchen.'

One step was taken and Mitch moved fluidly to block her way. An arm was stretched out to rest a hand on the garage wall to obstruct one avenue of retreat while the length of his body took care of the second. Behind Susan was the work counter and to one side was the wall. She was very effectively trapped.

'Will you please step out of my way?' But there was a betraying tremor in her voice.

'Bribe me.' The grooves around his mouth deepened, faint dimpling lines appearing in his lean cheeks.

Susan swallowed nervously and took a step backward. Mitch didn't follow. He didn't have to because there was nowhere she could go to escape him.

'Let me through, please.' It sounded more like a plea than the order she had intended to issue.

'Warren will never know I stole one of your kisses from him unless you tell him,' Mitch reasoned, flashing her one of those devastating smiles that made her heart turn over. 'What's the harm in one kiss? Neither of you will miss it.'

'No!' Susan made a small, negative movement with her head, not taking her wary eyes from him.

In her mind, she was considering the chances of successfully pushing her way past him. His movements to stop her would have to be hampered by his injuries.

As if reading her mind, Mitch spoke softly. 'It would be a shame if that pretty dress you have got soiled by this combination of grease, oil and dirt. Then you'd have to change clothes and make poor Warren wait. You have a choice, Beautiful. You can try to force your way by me, in which case I'll simply take my kiss. Or you can willingly give it to me and not get all messed up.'

'You are a blackmailer,' she accused in a low, taut voice.

The wicked glint in his eyes only grew brighter. 'Which is it to be?'

Wildly Susan searched for a third alternative and couldn't find one. With snapping fire in her brown eyes, she stepped toward him. Mitch obligingly bent his head, a suppressed smile of mockery grooved in his cheeks. Lightly she brushed the warmth of his lips with her own and withdrew immediately.

The golden brown head moved to the side in patient despair. 'I said a kiss, not a brotherly peck,' he scolded mockingly.

Susan breathed in sharply. 'That isn't fair!'

'I haven't time to play fair. Are you going to do it right?' Now the blue eyes were daring her to kiss him, silently chiding that she didn't have the nerve.

Nibbling uncertainly at her lower lip, Susan wondered if she did. Then she threw caution to the wind and moved toward him again. Her gaze scanned his handsome face, taking in again the challenging glitter in his brilliant blue eyes.

Her lashes fluttered down as her lips trembled against his mouth. Although she didn't draw away, it was still a mock kiss, a stiff touching that only outwardly resembled a kiss.

'Like this, honey,' Mitch said against her lips.

His mouth close warmly over hers, melting the rigidity that had held Susan back. The soft persuasion of his kiss had her yielding before she realized what she was doing, and by then the sensations rushing through her were too firmly in command to try to check.

The sweet possession of his mouth had her reeling. Her hands spread themselves against his chest to steady herself. The beginnings of a fiery response had just started to be offered when a door opened.

The sound brought Susan sharply back to reality as she realized what she was doing. Quickly she pushed herself away from Mitch, her head jerking toward the rear garage door. Her fear-widened eyes met Greg's stunned expression before swinging with accusing embarrassment to Mitch's calm face.

A faintly triumphant smile touched the sensual male lips that had seconds before rocked her common sense. Mitch returned his outstretched arm to his side and stepped back to let her go by him. She stalked angrily away from him.

'Wow,' Greg whistled. 'Wait until old Warren finds out about this!'

Susan stopped in front of her brother, tears of shame and frustration gathering in her eyes and turning them liquid brown. 'If you say one word of this to Warren, Gregory Allen Mabry, so help me I'll ...'

But no suitably chastising threat came to mind. Her mouth snapped shut and her trembling legs carried her swiftly to the connecting kitchen door.

The memory of that kiss haunted Susan for days. Each time she saw Mitch after that her gaze unwillingly strayed to the firm masculine lips, and again the impact of their touch would flood through her. It was frightening to remember her physical reaction to the essentially forced kiss.

What was worse, Mitch knew she had been disturbed by his kiss. The light in his eyes reminded Susan of it every time he looked at her, although she made certain no occasion occurred that would leave her alone in a room with Mitch.

If only she could explain to herself the strange ambivalence of her emotions. She was engaged to a man she loved and respected, yet she had experienced physical desire for another man. How was it possible?

She sighed dispiritedly.

'What's the matter, darling?' Warren probed softly.

'Hmm? She glanced at him blankly, forgetting for a few minutes where she was and whom she was with. She shook her head slightly, his question sinking in. 'Oh, nothing. Just tired, I guess.'

'You've been preoccupied nearly all week,' he commented, turning the car into the driveway of her home and switching off the engine.

'Nonsense,' Susan lied with a shrugging smile as she moved contentedly into his arms when he half turned in his seat.

His mouth closed masterfully over hers. It was an experienced kiss meant to arouse the response that it did. But Susan was disappointed again at the lack of chemical combustion. An ache throbbed painfully in her heart because she couldn't stop herself from comparing Warren's kisses with Mitch's. It wasn't right to do it and she hated herself for it.

'I wish I didn't have to go in,' she murmured as he nuzzled the lobe of her ear.

'You're certainly having trouble making up your mind,' Warren spoke in a curiously amused tone. 'A minute ago you said you were tired and now you say you wish you didn't have to go in.' He drew his head away, gazing at her intently. 'That Indy guy hasn't been bothering you, has he?'

'Oh, Warren, don't be silly,' Susan denied with a brittle laugh. 'Of course he hasn't.'

'Well, he'd better not.' The unspoken threat was obvious and Susan shifted uncomfortably in his arms. 'Come on. It's after one o'clock,' Warren announced. 'You'd better be getting in the house or else you'll find yourself getting ready for Sunday morning church without any sleep.'

He didn't allow Susan an opportunity to express her opinion as he moved her out of his embrace and stepped from the car. She stared at the darkened windows of the house and wondered how she was going to get through the whole of tomorrow—no, today it was now—with Mitch underfoot all the time.

Still silently considering that problem, she accepted Warren's hand out of the car and walked to the front door nestled under the crook of his arm. At the door, he stopped and turned her into his arms.

'I wish we were already married,' Susan sighed wistfully as she raised her head for his goodnight kiss. 'Why do we have to wait until August, darling? Why don't we get married now, in June?'

'Because we've already made all our plans with the intention of getting married in August,' he said patiently. 'Father will be fully recovered by then and I'll be able to take time off for our honeymoon. Besides, all our friends know of our plans. I respect you too much, Susan, to suddenly throw our plans aside and elope. That would raise too many eyebrows.'

'I suppose so,' she agreed submissively, and knew she had only been seeking a coward's way out of her dilemma. Mitch would be leaving before the month was out anyway and he would be taking that fleeting physical attraction she felt with him. It was only a matter of time.

'Good night, darling' Warren kissed her tenderly.

'Good night,' she whispered when he released her and walked to the car.

She stood in front of the door, lifting a hand in farewell as he reversed out of the drive. Then she reached for the doorknob, the door unlocked as she knew it would be.

Stepping inside, she closed the door and leaned against it for a few weary seconds. She breathed in deeply and exhaled a long sigh before straightening and turning to lock the night-bolts. They had just clicked into place when someone rapped lightly on the door.

Susan froze. 'Who is it?'

'It's me,' a quiet voice answered. 'Mitch.'

Quickly unlocking the door, she opened it, staring at him with curious wariness. He was leaning lazily with one arm propped against the door frame. Her brows drew together when he failed to walk in.

'What are you doing out there?' she asked.

'Walking and thinking.' Susan thought she detected a weariness in his voice. 'I wouldn't have bothered you except that I was afraid you would lock me out. I would hate to wake up the whole household in the middle of the night so someone could let me in.'

Glancing at the navy shirt that matched the check of his slim-fitting trousers, Susan noticed that he had worked the long sleeves over the cast on his left arm although it was still held in a sling.

'It's awfully late,' she said with faint curiosity.

'I wasn't waiting up for you, if that's what you're thinking,' Mitch smiled wryly. 'I couldn't sleep. My arm was bothering me too much. Healing pains, I guess.'

'Oh,' Susan offered in a tiny voice. 'Would you ... would you like me to get you something for it?'

'You mean a pain pill? No, thanks,' he refused. 'The pain isn't so bad that I can't endure it. It's a beautiful night. I'll just wander around out here for a while and see if I can't take my mind off it.' He straightened from the door, the moonlight glistening with a silvery sheen on his brown hair.

Sympathy surfaced instantly. 'Are you sure there's nothing I can do?' Susan offered.

Mitch hesitated. 'Well, you could——-' Then he shook his head and stepped away. 'No, never mind. You wouldn't want to anyway. Don't lock me out, Susan. Goodnight.'

'Wait,' she called hesitantly. 'Was there something I could do?'

He shrugged slightly. 'I was going to ask if you would want to walk with me for a while, just so I could have someone to talk to instead of thinking about this throbbing in my arm. But I know you're probably thinking that I had something else in mind. I know you don't trust me, so let's just forget about it.'

'What would we talk about?' she asked.

Mitch looked back at her. The expression on the handsomely tanned face was solemn and serious. There was no mockery, not even a suggestion of it lurking anywhere near the surface.

'We could compare the new Offy with the Cosworth engine,' he stated indifferently, 'or the price of tea in China. It doesn't matter, Susan. Forget I mentioned it.'

'We would just talk?' she asked for his confirmation of his earlier statement again.

'I won't promise that, Susan,' Mitch sighed heavily. 'With you, I never know from one minute to the next. Right now all I can think about is the needles stabbing my arm. If you want to walk with me, then all right, let's go. If not—well, I understand why and we'll forget it.'

'I'll come,' she said quietly, and stepped through the door, shutting it behind her, 'for a while,' she qualified.

'I'll try to behave,' Mitch smiled faintly with a half-promise.

It was a warm summer's night, quiet and lazy. Midnight dew glistened with tiny diamond drops on the grass and leaves. Crickets chirruped in somnolent competition with the cicadas in the trees. The houses lining the streets were dark. There wasn't a moving thing in sight.

Stars shimmered softly, sprinkled over the nearly black sky. The moon, lopsided in three-quarter stage, was a pale gold, changing to silver.

In a mutually agreed silence, Susan and Mitch wandered into the back yard where the spreading limbs of a maple tree shaded Beth Mabry's rose garden. Beneath a thick limb was a bench swing, ivory white in the night shade. The scent of roses filled the air.

Susan chose one side of the swing and Mitch the other with a comfortable space in between. 'You were right,' she murmured. The quietness was so peaceful that it seemed almost wrong to break it. 'It is a beautiful night.'

'Thank you. I ordered it specially.' Mitch leaned back, an absent smile curving his mouth as he gazed through the maple leaves to the night sky.

'Specially for what?' Susan countered.

'For sleepless nights.' The swing rocked gently as he shifted into a more comfortable position, easing the arm sling on to his lap. 'Talk to me about something, Susan.'

'What about?' she responded uncertainly.

Mitch slid a sideways glance at her, his mouth curving slightly. 'Tell me what it's like to grow up a doctor's daughter.'

It was her turn to smile faintly. 'I doubt if it's any different. My childhood was very normal.'

But she sensed that it was words he wanted to hear to distract his thoughts from the pain of his knitting arm. He was hurting. She could tell by the stiffness of the smile he had given her a second ago. It had been an absent, almost indifferent movement of his mouth without the warmth it usually reflected.

'Begin at the beginning, then,' Mitch instructed, 'with your very normal entry into the world.'

'Well let's see.' Susan leaned back in the swing, staring into the night sky as Mitch was doing. 'The stork brought me the first year that Mom and Dad were married. Dad was still in college. He hadn't begun his postgraduate work in medical school yet. My unplanned arrival on the scene was a hardship for them, I know. But Mom said she never regretted having me. She said she didn't know what she would have done if I hadn't been around to keep her company when Dad was putting in those long hours of internship. She worked, of course, and the landlady, a Mrs. Gibson, took care of me. Greg arrived the year Dad started his own practice. Amy came four years later.'

His eyes were closed when she looked at him. Susan wondered if he was asleep or merely resting. Then Mitch spoke to fill the silent pause.

'I was certain I was going to hear about all the contests you won as a baby,' he mocked lightly without lifting the spiky fan of lashes. 'You had to have been teacher's pet at school.'

'Pet or pest?' Susan laughed softly.

Quietly she began to relate anecdotes of her childhood in school and at home. While she talked, she studied him. His closed eyes kept her inspection safe from discovery.

In repose, his face—minus crinkling laughter around his eyes and the dimpling lines in the smooth lean cheeks—was still extraordinarily handsome. The roguish air, associated with a playboy, was gone.

Indomitable strength was roughly and arrogantly carved in Warren's features. Mitch Braden possessed the same strength, but in him it was tempered with determination and consideration. Mitch did not overpower people with the force of his personality. He charmed them to his side.

Concluding a story about a pet rabbit she had received one Easter, Susan noticed his breathing had become quite even and how relaxed his posture had become.

'Mitch?' she murmured.

'Yes,' he answered in a clear, quiet voice.

'I thought my talk might have bored you into falling asleep,' she explained, directing the wryly amused tone of voice at herself.

Mitch opened his eyes, blue and jewel-bright, focusing his gaze unerringly on her face. Steadily he looked at her.

'I don't think there's anything about you that would bore me, Susan,' he replied quite seriously.

Unnerved by the smooth way he had countered her jesting comment with a disturbing compliment, Susan turned away. The atmosphere of moonlight and roses was too romantic for her to be completely untouched by his statement.

'It's your turn now to tell me about yourself,' she said, trying to change the subject.

'What do you want to know?' Mitch inquired curiously. 'Shall I tell you of all the snips and snails and puppydog tails I collected as a mischievous boy?'

Susan didn't want to know about his childhood. She was reluctant to hear about the personal details of his past life. It was better not to learn too much about him.

'Tell me about racing.' She chose a safer topic. 'Why do you do it?'

'That's like asking why a man climbs a mountain or why a matador enters the bullring,' he chuckled softly at her question. 'It's the constant challenge, I suppose.'

'What's it like to drive in a race?'

He considered her question for several seconds before answering. 'Your heart pounds to send adrenalin surging through your system and your senses are more alert than you can ever remember. It's the high level of energy that sustains you when the gravity force exerted on you in the turns tries to pull you apart. It keeps you going when you're so bone weary and exhausted that you want to drop. There's a crazy kind of peace and freedom you feel when you're out there on the track. I don't know where it comes from,' he mused thoughtfully. 'It isn't from the cheering of the crowd or the deafening roar of a powerful engine. It isn't even from being the first car over the finish line. It comes from inside, I guess. You are competing with yourself, driving yourself to the limit of what you can endure, then discovering you can go farther.'

'Aren't you ever frightened?' Susan asked, suddenly fascinated by the insight into a sport she had never really considered in such a philosophical way.

'A man would be a fool if he didn't admit to being aware of the danger and the risks,' Mitch smiled. 'But you don't have time to be frightened, not at the speed you are traveling. By the time your mind can concentrate on the thing that frightens you, whether it's a particularly steep bank or the car ahead of you that's gone out of control, you're already past it or the worst has happened.'

His calm acceptance of the hazards made Susan shiver. Her heart was in her throat just visualizing Mitch in a race. There was the instinctive knowledge that she would live with fear if she ever watched him race.

'I think it's time we went into the house,' Mitch announced. 'It's beginning to get cool, and you must be tired.'

Susan didn't correct his assumption that her shiver had been from the growing coolness of the night air. She accepted the hand he offered to help her out of the swing.

'How is your arm?' she asked. 'Is it still bothering you?' 'Hardly at all now.' A lazy smile spread across his features, crinkling the corners of his eyes. 'Thanks to you.'

Mitch didn't release her hand as they retraced their steps to the front of the house. The warmth of his grip was comforting as if he was silently assuring her not to worry about him.

8

Inside the house, Mitch released her hand and turned to lock the front door. Susan waited for him a few steps inside. She didn't know why except that it seemed the polite thing to do.

'Are you tired?' he glanced at her inquiringly.

'A little,' she admitted. 'Aren't you?'

'Unfortunately, no.' His shoulders lifted in a rueful gesture. 'Do you suppose your mother would object if I fixed myself some cocoa? I can't stand hot milk.'

'Of course she wouldn't mind.' Susan hesitated, then admitted, 'I'll fix it for you, if you like.'

There was a merry sparkle in his look. 'To tell you the truth, I was hoping you'd volunteer. I didn't like the idea of having to poke through the cupboards trying to find things. You'll join me, won't you?'

The boyish honesty and engaging smile were too much for Susan to combat. Besides, although she was tired, she wasn't ready for the evening to end. She didn't want to examine the reason for that thought too closely.

'Yes, I'll join you,' she agreed 'Do you want to have it in the kitchen or shall I bring it into the living room?'

'The kitchen is fine. We'll be less likely to disturb the others there.' Mitch started for the hallway leading to the kitchen. 'I'll give you a hand. Of course I only have one hand that I can use.'

In the kitchen, Susan put the milk on to heat and stirred in the cocoa and sugar. She pointed out the cupboard where Mitch could find the mugs and another one where the marshmallows were kept.

As the cocoa mixture began to simmer, Susan glanced over her shoulder at Mitch. He was walking toward her, carrying the two mugs by a finger curled through the handles.

'There are sugar cookies in the cookie jar if you want a snack,' she offered.

'No, thanks,' he refused, and watched as she carefully poured the hot chocolate into the mugs and floated a pair of marshmallows on the hot liquid in each mug.

They each carried their own cup to the narrow breakfast table in front of the glassed windows looking into the back yard. Mitch waited as Susan sat down in the chair at the head of the table, then he took the chair to her left.

'How long have you known Warren?' he asked casually.

'Why?' Susan tipped her head to one side, surprised by his unexpected question.

'Just curious,' Mitch shrugged.

Susan couldn't think of any reason not to answer his question. 'I was formally introduced to him when I went to work for the law firm in the secretarial pool. Two years ago I became his personal secretary when his previous one left to get married.'

'That's quite a long courtship, isn't it?' he grinned crookedly.

'Oh, no,' she hurried to explain. 'We didn't start dating until after the Christmas party last year.'

'Not until then?' he frowned in faint disbelief.

'Well, Warren didn't actually notice me as more than his secretary until then.' She sipped self-consciously at her steaming cocoa.

'The man must have been blind,' he laughed in short disbelief. 'What about you? Had you noticed him?'

Susan stirred the melting marshmallows into her hot chocolate. 'Secretaries are always in love with their bosses without their bosses being aware of it.' She tried to make it a joke, unable to meet the mocking glint in Mitch's eyes. 'I thought everybody knew that.'

'And after the Christmas party, it was a case of love at first and very late sight for Warren, is that it?' Mitch inquired with decided cynicism. 'I mean, you already believed you were half in love with him.'

'I guess it was like that,' Susan admitted nervously.

'Then how long have you been engaged?'

'Since April.'

'April Fools' Day?' he asked mockingly.

There was a defiant tilt of her chin. 'He gave me the ring over the Easter weekend, if you must know.'

'I would have thought you would have planned a traditional June wedding,' Mitch gazed thoughtfully at the cup in his hand, 'instead of waiting until August. But then I guess the idea to marry then wasn't yours.'

Warily Susan studied his bland expression, a thought just occurring to her and one that she probably should have had earlier.

'You were hiding somewhere listening to Warren and me tonight, weren't you?' she accused in a low, angry voice.

'Inadvertently,' he admitted without apology. 'I didn't intentionally eavesdrop. I heard the car drive in and assumed it was you. I wanted to be certain you didn't lock me out of the house. Warren usually doesn't walk you to the door, or at least he hasn't lately.'

Susan remembered suddenly that the guest bedroom that Mitch used had a clear view of the front door. He must have been spying on her ever since he had come.

'You could have let us know you were there,' she retorted bitterly trying to remember what she and Warren had said.

'The topic sounded very personal. I didn't think either of you would appreciate my opinion on the matter,' Mitch explained, the wicked glitter back in his blue eyes. 'Does he make love to you?'

The spoon clattered from her hand on to the table. Fire flashed in her eyes.

'If you're asking whether I sleep with him, then you're just going to have to wonder, because I have no intention of answering such an objectionable question!'

'Temper, temper, Susan!' He clicked his tongue at her in mock reproval. 'Obviously the man doesn't.'

'Obviously?' she echoed angrily. 'Why obviously?'

'There are several things that made me reach that conclusion,' Mitch answered lazily. 'You might have wanted to set the wedding date ahead because you were becoming frustrated sexually. And everything is so precise between the two of you. Certain nights you have dates. On the week nights he has you home at a certain hour. Everything fits into a prim pattern. Believe me, Warren isn't a man overcome with passion. He's doing everything by the book, including waiting until the wedding night.'

Trembling, Susan stared at him while he casually drank his cocoa. 'You sound as if that's something to be ashamed of!' she accused.

'Of course not,' Mitch denied with a deprecating laugh. 'But wouldn't you feel better if his control broke just once? Wouldn't it make him a little more human?'

'I don't know what you're talking about.' She looked away hastily, staring at the foamy residue clinging to the sides of her mug. 'Besides, Warren is in love with me, whether you want to believe it or not.'

'In his way, yes,' he nodded agreeably.

'What do you mean by that?' she asked with an irritated sigh.

'If I were a girl engaged to a man and that man held me in his arms and declared how very much he respected me, I would be insulted,' he answered simply.

'I see.' Her fingers drummed a war beat on the table top. 'What you're really saying is that you wouldn't respect the woman you married. Isn't that right, Mr. Braden?'

'Naturally I would respect her, or I wouldn't marry her.' Mitch met the angry glitter of her gaze with good-humored patience. 'But that certainly isn't the emotion I would want to feel when I held her in my arms.'

'No, I suppose you would feel lust,' Susan retorted sarcastically.

'Why not? I'm a lusty man.' Amusement touched his mouth, her barbs bouncing off without inflicting one prick.

'I think you're impossible!' she declared with a frustrated shake of her head as she looked away.

Out of the corner of her eye, she saw him rub the back of his neck, with a slight stretching motion of his shoulders. 'And because I would enjoy making love to the woman I want to marry, that makes me impossible?' he chided.

'You make it sound as if it's all your decision,' Susan replied. 'I should think the girl might have something to say about it.'

'If she loved me, she would be willing.' His hand moved to wearily rub his mouth and chin. Susan's stifled gasp of indignant outrage drew his gaze from the mug to her. 'You don't believe me, do you?'

'I think that statement smacks of conceit!'

'Maybe,' Mitch acknowledged nonchalantly. 'But if I were Warren and you professed to love me as much as you say you love him, and if I chose to take advantage of that love—which I admit is what I would be doing—then I could have you in bed with me within twenty minutes and you wouldn't have made a single word or gesture of protest.'

'Of all the———' Susan sputtered.

But Mitch wasn't listening. His hand was covering a yawn that brought a watery brightness to his eyes. When it was over, he glanced at Susan, sending her a sheepishly rueful grin.

'That's a boastful statement to make, isn't it, for a man who's too tired to back it up,' he said with half a sigh. 'I guess the hot chocolate did the trick.'

Pushing the chair from the table, he rose to his feet and carried his empty coffee mug to the sink. Susan stared angrily at him for a few seconds, then picked up her own mug and followed him.

'Would you like me to help clean up?' Mitch offered when she shoved her mug in the sink and walked stiffly to the stove for the pan.

'No thanks,' she snapped.

He stood beside the sink, a hip leaning against the counter, and watched the suppressed anger in her movements. But Susan refused to meet his gaze.

'I upset you, Susan,' he said slowly. 'That wasn't my intention. I should have been thanking you for so considerately spending some time with me. Instead I started needling you about your engagement to Warren. I was jealous—I still am. I suppose that's why I was so brash. I'm sorry, truly.'

Susan stood in front of the sink, the pot nervously clutched in her hands. She was aware of his gaze studying her bent head. The sincerity in his voice had taken away most of her outraged anger. She swallowed down the lump in her throat.

Why did he constantly have to confuse her? One minute she was trembling with anger at his taunts and another she would be feeling the force of his attraction. Part of her liked the idea that Mitch was attracted to her and showed it, while the other half was indignant that she should feel that way when she was already engaged to marry another man.

'I accept your apology,' she said tightly, not ready to wholeheartedly forgive him for provoking her so. She glanced at the wall clock above the sink. 'It's a minute after two. You need some sleep.'

'Are you positive you don't want me to help with those dishes?' Mitch repeated his offer, still trying to catch her downcast gaze.

'I'm only going to stack them in the sink and wipe off the counter and stove. I can manage that on my own, thank you.' Her clipped voice was deliberately cool and indifferent.

His hand closed over her chin, his grip firm but not harsh. He turned her head so he could look into her face. Resentment still smoldered in her dark eyes as she met the patient blueness of his.

'I'm sorry for making you angry, Susan.'

'So you said.'

'And I want to thank you again for keeping me company tonight. I appreciate it,' Mitch finished in a level, serious tone. Then he leaned forward and lightly touched his lips to hers. 'Good night.'

Her chin was released and he was walking away before Susan could offer a protest at his action. When the kitchen door closed behind him, she touched a fingertip to her lips. They still tingled with the warmth of his light caress.

Jerkily she brushed the dark hair away from her temple and set about the task of cleaning up, a minor one that hardly took any time. All the time she kept wondering how long it would be before this physical chemistry between her and Mitch would fizzle out. For the sake of her peace of mind it couldn't be too soon.

Two minutes after Mitch had left the kitchen, Susan followed, making her way up the darkened stairs to the unlit hallway of the second floor. Unerringly she turned in the direction of the bathroom to clean off her makeup and brush her teeth before changing into night clothes. Her steps took her past the guest bedroom.

From inside came a stifled gasp of pain and a few savagely muttered oaths. Her eyes darted curiously to the strip of light beneath the door just as it swung open to catch her in full light.

Mitch's tall frame was in the center of the doorway, his navy blue long-sleeved shirt unbuttoned. He started to stride into the hallway, saw Susan and stopped, a dark frown on his forehead.

'Give me a hand, would you?' It was a crisp demand rather than a request as he pivoted around to reenter his room. 'I can't get my shirt off with this cast on my arm.'

Susan hesitated in the hallway, watching as Mitch impatiently tried to shrug his right arm out of the long sleeve. He glanced over his shoulder, the look in his eyes asking her what she was doing still standing in the hall.

'If you'd hold the sleeve, I think I can pull my arm out of it,' he said with a thin thread of patience.

His struggle to remove the shirt was genuine and Susan walked into his room to help. She held the sleeve while he twisted his arm, grunting once with pain.

'Now all I have to do is work the other sleeve over my cast,' he muttered, tossing her a disgruntled look. 'And to think all this is because I was tired of dangling sleeves!'

'Let me help with that,' Susan offered, stepping around to his other side to ease the shirt off the cast. 'It will be easier, I think, if we take your arm out of the sling to begin with.'

Mitch slipped his arm out of the cradle sling. Together they worked the sleeve material over the plaster cast until his was free.

It was difficult for Susan not to look at his naked torso. His chest was as tanned as the rest of him, muscles rippling sinewy strong with curling tawny gold hair sprinkled over the center of his smooth chest. The flat stomach and slim waist belonged to an athlete.

'Shouldn't you be wearing an elastic support for those cracked ribs of yours?' she questioned, self-consciously turning away to drape his shirt over a chair.

'You mean my corset.' His mouth quirked mockingly. 'It became more of an irritant then a help, so I took it off.'

'I see,' she murmured, glancing in his direction without quite looking at him.

At this moment, his virility was like a bright fire on a cold Indiana winter night, drawing her irresistibly to its warmth. Susan forced her disturbed senses to the rear. She stood nervously before him, not wanting to leave and knowing she didn't dare stay. 'Would you like me to help you with your pajama top?'

A naughty light danced gleefully in his blue eyes. 'I don't mean to embarrass you, but I don't sleep in pajamas.'

'Oh,' she murmured, disconcerted by the image that sprang into her mind. Lowering her gaze she noticed the sling strap had become twisted around his neck. Without thinking, she reached upward to straighten it before Mitch slipped his arm into the cradle sling. Her fingers felt icily cold compared to the fire that seemed to burn beneath his skin.

The top of her head felt the caressing warmth of his breath near it. Her lashes veiled much of her disturbed state as she looked into his eyes. A mask seemed to have been pulled over the brilliant blue, yet the directness of his gaze compelled her not to glance away.

With a certainty that frightened her, she knew she wanted Mitch to kiss her. Her hands had completed their task, but they remained lightly touching the back of his neck. His hand was resting casually on the side of her waist.

'Susan.' There was a question in his husky, caressing voice.

'Yes?' she answered, her lips parting in invitation.

Mitch slowly lowered his head toward her, prolonging the moment when their lips met as if he expected her to deny the kiss at the last second and was allowing her time to protest.

A convulsive shudder quaked through Susan at the tentative possession. His mouth moved mobilely over hers, tasting the sweetness of her lips. The stiffness, the unnamed fear began to leave her body, melting under his gentle kiss.

The hardness of the plaster cast was behind her back while his right hand lightly caressed her waist and shoulder. When he released her mouth to begin an exploring search of her face and neck, Susan kept her face upturned, eyes closed by the magic in his touch.

A sigh of longing broke from her lips an instant before he claimed them again. This time it was with firm possession, a long, drugging kiss that stole her breath and awakened her senses that she had held in limbo.

Her hands twined themselves around his neck, not needing the pressure of his hands to mold herself against his length. Arching against him, she was subconsciously aware of his muscular thighs and the solidity of his bare chest. The knowledge added itself to the buffeting storm of emotions raging inside her, sensations that Susan had never experienced before.

Reeling under the turbulent winds that rocked her, she wasn't conscious of movement under Mitch's guiding hands. The action seemed part of the whirlwind that claimed her, the result of the hardening passion in his kiss.

Then there was a strange floating sensation. Her legs no longer needed to support her. Again his mouth began exploring the sensitive hollow of her throat, drawing tiny gasps of bewildered, sensuous pleasure from deep within. His fingers spread over the naked skin of her back, igniting fresh sparks with their caress. Absently Susan acknowledged that he must have loosened her blouse from her skirt.

'Now do you see what I mean, darling?' Mitch murmured against her throat.

Her lashes blinked with confusion at the smoldering blueness of his half-closed eyes.

'Mean about what?' Susan whispered blankly. The throbbing ache in her voice begged for the words to stop and the kisses to continue.

'Seventeen minutes. That's all it took,' he answered complacently.

'Seventeen minutes?' she repeated, trying to rise above the storm that had made everything so topsy-turvy.

'This is the way it should be, my beautiful one,' he stated decisively, and leaned his head forward to nuzzle her ear.

A frown puckered her forehead as the cyclonic upheaval began to recede. A stark white cloth was behind Mitch's head. In disbelief she stared at it, then at the maple headboard of the bed inches away.

'I could have you in bed with me in twenty minutes.' The words came back with slapping force. Mitch had said that in the kitchen not—seventeen minutes ago.

Horror washed over her head as she suddenly realized what he was talking about.

'How could you do this!' she breathed with fear-widened eyes.

'Do what?' he asked with mocking indifference.

'You tried to seduce me!' she accused. The pliancy was gone as she held herself rigid under his continued caress.

'If that had been my intention, darling, you would already have been seduced,' Mitch chuckled softly.

'How dare you!' she choked on a bubble of righteous indignation.

His arms tightened when she tried to pull away. Struggling and twisting, she succeeded in breaking away from his embrace, uncaring of the muffled cry of pain Mitch made as she accidentally hit his injured ribs.

'What's the matter with you?' he muttered as he tried to follow her.

'You can ask me that!' Frantically, she pushed the end of her blouse into the waistband of her skirt.

'Darling—'

'Don't you darling me!' snapped Susan.

'Keep your voice down,' he frowned, but with considerable amusement.

'I'll talk just as loudly as I please.' Yet she spoke in a softer and more angry tone.

'Susan,' Mitch murmured, in a coaxing, placating voice meant to soothe her growing temper.

'You lured me into your room deliberately just to prove your point, didn't you?' she accused.

'Not exactly,' he hedged. 'I suppose I could have eventually fought my way out of that shirt, but I admit I did use it to persuade you to come in.'

'I suppose you're going to try to convince me now that it was a practical joke,' she hissed. 'You have a very warped sense of humor, Mitch Braden!'

He was standing in front of her now, easily within reaching distance, but his hand remained on his hip, a mocking kind of patience in his handsome features.

'My full name is Mitchum Alexander Braden,' he told her. 'My mother always liked to use all of it when she was really angry with me.'

'Well, I'm angry, too, Mitchum Alexander Braden!' she declared with some satisfaction. 'I think it was a mean, contemptible trick you played when you knew I'm engaged to Warren!'

'That is precisely my point in this,' Mitch drawled. 'You aren't in love with him. I tricked you because I was running out of time to prove that you don't love him. You have to realize it before you do something you'll live to regret, like marrying him.'

'You're quite wrong.'

'I am?' he said with challenging humor. 'Tell me how you love him so much that you can almost allow *me* to seduce you?'

'Did it ever occur to you that I might have been imagining Warren in your place?' Susan retorted with some fast thinking.

'No, it didn't occur to me, and it doesn't now,' Mitch replied. 'You're only saying that to try to salvage some of your pride. Don't be stubborn by refusing to admit to yourself the truth of what I'm saying.'

'Truth! The truth is that I want you to leave me alone!'

'You're angry right now, Susan,' Mitch sighed. 'Think about what I've said, would you?'

His hand reached toward her and fell to his side as she took a hasty step away. Without saying another word, Susan turned around and walked swiftly from his room.

Several minutes later she was in her own bed, staring at the ceiling. How had she allowed herself to be tricked into that embarrassing situation? Nothing Mitch had said had been true. He had jumped to erroneous conclusions, she assured herself.

She was in love with Warren. She had loved him for almost two years. After that much time, a person didn't stop loving someone in one night.

'Not unless,' a little voice said, 'you never loved him in the beginning.'

'Impossible!' Susan whispered aloud, jamming a fist into her pillow and turning on her side.

9

'Susan, are you going to sleep until noon or are you going to get up?' Amy demanded impatiently, jiggling her sleeping sister's shoulder.

'W-what?' Groggily Susan blinked open her eyes, absently brushing away the hand on her shoulder.

'Mom has breakfast ready. Are you coming down or not?'

'Yes.' She snuggled deeper into her pillow. Then she realized the action would only bring more sleep and stretched out of her comfortable position. 'I'll get dressed and be right down.'

Amy waited until she saw her sister throw the covers off before she left the room. A gloomy sense of depression seemed to be clinging to Susan as she reached for the cranberry robe draped over a chair. As she slipped her arms into the sleeves, she remembered last night and the depression grew darker.

How was she going to face Mitch after the way she had behaved, she wondered, as she slid her feet into terrycloth slippers. Where had her common sense been? What could she say to him that would convince him it had all been a mistake?

Mistake! It had been a catastrophe. She simply had to convince him that she didn't want anything more to do with him. But how?

Plagued by her seemingly unsolvable dilemma, Susan ran a hand through her sleep-tousled hair. She stared sightlessly at the carpeted floor of the hallway as she made her way to the bathroom.

Opposite Mitch's room, her gaze nervously strayed to the open door. The room was empty. From downstairs, she could hear voices of her family and guessed that he was down there with them.

Breathing a sigh of relief that their moment of confrontation had been put off, Susan turned toward the open bathroom door. She stopped short inside its frame. Mitch was standing in front of the mirror above the sink, shirtless as he had been last night but wearing a pair of wheat tan pants instead of the blue checked.

Before she could recover from her surprise and retreat, the fingers of his right hand closed over her wrist and drew her into the room. When she pulled to free herself from his hold, he released her immediately. The movement of his hand continued fluidly to close the door.

'Good morning, Beautiful,' he smiled lazily, his eyes moving possessively over her face. 'I didn't think it was possible, but you're even more beautiful first thing in the morning.'

'I imagine you've seen a lot of women "first thing in the morning"!' she snapped sarcastically, saying the first thing that came to her mind.

'I do believe you're jealous,' he chuckled. 'That's good.'

'That's absurd!' she denied with an impatient toss of her head away from his handsome face. 'You're so determined to see everything the way you want it to be that there isn't any use trying to explain things to you. Excuse me.'

'Wait.' His hand reached out again, checking her movement to leave. Susan stared pointedly at the fingers on her arm. 'Would you help me a second?'

She warily raised her eyes to his face.

Mitch smiled crookedly. 'No tricks, I promise.'

'What do you want?' she asked, still not trusting him.

'I've been trying for the last ten minutes to pour some after-shave lotion in my hand and I'm fast running out of patience,' he explained.

Her gaze found the uncapped bottle of aftershave lotion sitting on the counter beside the washbasin. That much of his statement seemed to be true.

He let go of her arm and reached for the bottle, tucking it in a precarious position between his cast and his body, cupping his right hand near the top of the bottle.

'You see what I mean,' he said as he tried to tip his body to one side to allow the liquid to run into his hand and nearly dropped the bottle in the process.

Sighing, Susan took the bottle from him and poured a small quantity in his hand, which he quickly rubbed over his freshly shaven face.

His gaze danced to her impassive expression. 'I thought you might have wanted to put it on. It would have given you a chance to slap my face.'

'Would it have done any good?' she asked cuttingly.

'You're still upset about last night, aren't you?' The crinkling lines around his eyes smoothed out as his expression became gently serious.

Her pulse began behaving erratically under his level gaze. 'I don't wish to discuss it with you.'

'I've backed you into a corner, haven't I, Susan?' he shrugged ruefully. 'And all I meant to do was to bring you out in the open where you could see things for yourself.'

His hand lightly caressed her cheek as he tucked a wayward strand of dark hair behind her ear. His hand remained there cupping the side of her head. Susan felt an inexplicable urge to turn her face into his hand and kiss his palm.

Why did he have to be so gentle? She could have withstood his mockery and his flattery. But this? Her eyes misted a liquid brown.

A thumb raised her chin. Too numbed by her inner bewilderment to protest, she remained motionless as his head bent toward her. His mouth lovingly caressed her trembling lips and that crazy whirlwind of emotions came sweeping over her again. It took all her strength to stand solidly in the face of it.

Finally, when Susan thought she could resist no longer, he raised his head, smiling lightly into her eyes with a tenderness as moving as his gentleness had been.

'When are you going to give Warren back his ring?' Mitch asked huskily.

Was there a faint unevenness to his breathing? Susan couldn't be certain. She stiffened away from the hand resting on her cheek.

'I'm not giving it back.' She lowered her gaze to the sling holding his arm. 'I'm going to marry him.'

'Susan, Susan,' Mitch sighed dispiritedly. 'When are you going to wake up?'

'When are you?' she demanded in a childishly hurt and confused voice. 'I keep telling you and telling you, but you won't listen. Why can't you leave me alone?'

'Is that what you really want me to do?' His eyes narrowed into piercing blue diamonds, cutting hard.

'Yes! Yes, it is!' Susan declared forcefully.

'All right.' His mouth tightened into an uncompromising line as he stepped away from her. 'If that's what you want, I will leave you alone.'

Without another word, Mitch walked out of the bathroom leaving Susan standing there more bewildered and uncertain than she had been a moment ago.

And Mitch kept his word. He left Susan alone.

It was no small accomplishment when they both lived in the same house. Yet he succeeded. Whenever Susan entered a room, he found an excuse to leave. At the evening meal, he avoided addressing any comment to her, however trivially. Never once had she caught him looking at her.

If the family noticed the way they ignored each other, none of them said anything to Susan. For them, life seemed to be going very much as usual.

But not for Susan. She kept reminding herself how wonderful it was that she had finally made Mitch leave her alone. In truth, she was restless, on edge, and troubled. She blamed the state on Mitch's presence in the house. When he finally left, then everything would be all right. But she couldn't quite convince herself of that.

Her three dates with Warren since Mitch had begun ignoring her hadn't proved to be very enjoyable. Each time he embraced her, Susan began comparing her reactions to what she had felt with Mitch. It became impossible to respond to his kisses when she was mentally checking her pulse and respiration rate.

Warren didn't help matters by constantly chiding her for being so nervous and restless. She had come very close several times to telling him to shut up and leave her alone, too. The whole situation was becoming ridiculous in the extreme.

The names on the wedding list blurred into a jumble of lines. Susan shook her head to clear her vision and tried to find where she had left off before she had become lost in thought.

'Hi!' Amy flounced down on the sofa cushion beside Susan. 'What are you doing?'

'Going over the invitation list for the wedding,' she sighed, running the eraser end of her pencil down the names, not certain which was the last name she had checked.

She wasn't really in the mood to do it, but it was something that needed to be done and it filled the time until she went to bed.

'Are you going to invite Mitch?' Amy asked eagerly.

Susan paused, the muscles in her stomach knotting at the mention of his name. 'I don't think Mitch would be very interested in coming to my wedding,' she replied, avoiding a direct answer.

'You would come, wouldn't you, Mitch, if Susan invited you?' Amy's inquiry was directed toward the hallway arch.

Glancing up in surprise, Susan bit into her lower lip. Mitch was standing in its frame, lazily watching her with an almost mocking expression in his eyes.

'It would be very difficult to refuse a written invitation from Susan,' he said dryly. 'That would practically be a milestone.'

Her eyes bounced away from his face to the papers on her lap. The cast had been removed from his left arm. Without the cumbersome protective cast, Mitch looked more vitally attractive than she remembered.

Susan couldn't think of a single reply she could make to his comment. She didn't want him at her wedding. Even though she didn't think he would come, she still didn't want to invite him.

Fortunately Amy filled the silence.

'I'm going to be one of Susan's bridesmaids.' Amy had declared vigorously that she was much too old to be a flower girl. 'I'm going to wear a beautiful long gown of emerald green. And Mother said I could go to a beautician and have her fix my hair on top of my head.'

'Johnny Chambers had better watch out if you catch that bridal bouquet,' he teased.

'Oh, Mitch!' Amy giggled, her cheeks turning nearly as red as her hair.

Susan knew that Johnny Chambers was one of the boys in Amy's class at school and also the object of her latest crush. Mitch was still her idol, though.

Mitch leisurely wandered into the room, pausing beside the sofa where Susan sat. Her hand trembled nervously as she felt him looking over her shoulder.

'Is that the list of guests you're inviting to the wedding?' he asked after several long seconds had passed.

'Actually,' Susan didn't let her gaze wander from the handwritten lists, 'what it is is my list and Warren's list. I have to compare the two to make certain we haven't duplicated any names.'

'Amy!' her mother called from another room. 'You've left your record albums strewn all over the family room. Come in here and pick them up before they get broken.'

'Oh, Mother!' Amy grumbled, and slid off the couch.

Shifting her leg uneasily, Susan waited for Mitch to leave. He had avoided her so completely in the past week that she was apprehensive about his reasons for staying.

'Susan.' He was asking for her attention, but she refused to look at him.

'Yes,' she said absently as if she had forgotten he was there.

'Are you really going through with this wedding?'

'Of course,' she laughed, pretending she didn't understand why he had asked that question. 'It would certainly be a waste of time to compile all these names if there wasn't going to be a wedding, wouldn't it?' She knew some kind of deflating retort would be forthcoming, so she didn't give him a chance to respond. 'I see the doctor removed your cast this afternoon. It must really be a relief not to have that weight on your arm,' Susan commented with forced nonchalance.

Out of the corner of her eye, she saw him absently flex his left arm as if testing it. 'Yes, it is a relief.' Mitch allowed the change of subject. 'The doctor said it was healing almost perfectly, and it certainly does feel better.'

'In a couple of weeks you'll be as good as new,' she observed brightly, still not letting her eyes stray from the paper on her lap.

'As good as new,' he agreed dryly. 'I'll be leaving next week, Susan.'

'So soon?' She flashed him a glance of surprise, meeting the watchfulness of his blue eyes. Then, feeling she had betrayed something, she immediately added, 'I imagine you're very eager to be on your way now that you've recovered.'

'Eager? I wouldn't say that,' he mocked. 'But I certainly don't have any reason not to meet the boys at Pocono now that the cast is off.'

'A-are you racing?' she frowned.

'I've entered in the Pocono 500 at the end of the month. The time trials start next week,' he told her.

A cold chill ran over her skin. She could hardly keep from shuddering. 'I—I'm sure you'll do very well,' she said. 'As Greg says, you're a very excellent driver.'

Mitch didn't reply to that rather inane comment. His head moved in a slight negative shake as if to say the situation was hopeless. In the next moment he was walking out of the room.

Be glad that he's leaving, Susan told herself. *Now everything will return to normal.* She could begin forgetting him. But there was an awful tightness in her throat.

When she mentioned Mitch's imminent departure to Warren the next night, he rejoiced openly with a scathing comment that it was about time. Susan's murmur of agreement was hollow. She tried, but she simply couldn't make herself be glad he was leaving.

Warren's exultation at the news forced her to hide the cloud of depression that had tagged along behind her ever since Mitch had told her.

Bright and early Wednesday morning was the time Mitch had chosen to leave, choosing the hour before Susan and her father left for work. Her mother cooked an enormous farewell breakfast, but most of the food Susan ate lodged itself somewhere between her throat and stomach.

She silently wished that Mitch had stolen away in the night, but he seemed determined to make his departure as big an impact on her life as his arrival had been.

Susan stayed in the kitchen helping her mother clear away the dishes rather than join Mitch's entourage. Her father, Greg, and Amy were all helping him pack the expensive blue sports car now parked in the driveway.

Finally there was no more to be done in the kitchen and Beth Mabry was urging her toward the outer door. Susan didn't want to take part in the lingering goodbye outside. She wished she were a child again so she could run away and hide. Instead she squared her shoulders and marched along beside her mother.

His few possessions were all stowed in the car. Mitch was leaning against the door when Susan and her mother joined the semicircle around him. His gaze touched her fleetingly before it casually moved away.

'Well,' Mitch drew a resigned breath and smiled as he straightened from the car and extended a hand to her father, 'I guess there isn't any reason to keep prolonging the moment when I have to say goodbye.'

'I wish you could, Mitch.' Simon Mabry gripped his hand firmly, a faint gruffness in his voice. 'We're going to miss you, all of us.'

'I can't say anything but thanks, and that doesn't seem like enough,' Mitch replied. He withdrew his hand and turned to her brother. 'Greg.'

Awkwardly Greg shook his hand. 'Good luck at Pocono. We'll be cheering for you.'

Amy's dark eyes were gazing at him soulfully when Mitch turned to her. She offered him her hand, a slight tremble in her chin.

'Goodbye, Mitch,' Amy said in a slightly strangled voice.

Mitch flashed one of those fulsome smiles that Susan had not seen in the last ten days. It was just as potent as it had always been and this time her sister was the object of his charm.

'May I kiss you goodbye, Amy?' he asked with an inquiring tilt of his head. 'I don't want Johnny Chambers to be the first.'

Amy's auburn head bobbed quickly in agreement, a sparkle of ecstatic disbelief in her eyes. Then Mitch was bending his head and tenderly brushing her sister's lips in a chaste kiss.

With her mother, Mitch didn't ask but kissed her lightly without speaking. Beth Mabry gave him a quick hug in return, a teary brightness appearing in her eyes.

'Thank you, Beth, for letting me be a part of your family for a while,' Mitch offered sincerely.

'We're going to miss you,' she reiterated her husband's statement.

The last one in the semicircle was Susan. She wanted to bolt and run when Mitch turned to her. For a long second he stood in front of her and said nothing, holding her troubled gaze with the compelling blueness of his.

The morning sun danced in his hair, brightening the shadowy brown. He looked so vigorous, so strong and so handsome that Susan felt her breath being ripped away. The image of him at this moment seemed to implant itself in her mind to be remembered and recalled for the rest of her life.

'And Susan,' he drawled, a faint smile turning up the corners of his mouth. 'I always try to save the best for last.'

The emotional scene leading up to this moment had eroded the control Susan had fought to attain. She had hoped to wish him a breezy goodbye and Godspeed. But the genuinely affectionate exchanges that had gone before had erased the barrier. Still, she tried.

'Goodbye, Mitch.' She spoke in a low tone so her voice wouldn't tremble and politely offered him her hand.

Mitch ignored her outstretched hand. 'Aren't you going to kiss me goodbye, Susan?' he asked with complete seriousness, not even the faintest glimmer of wicked mockery in his eyes.

Self-consciously she glanced to the amused expressions of her parents. She appeared to be the only one taken aback by his question. Her hand fell uncertainly to her side.

'Warren won't mind,' Mitch added, 'not since you're kissing me goodbye. You never know, we might never see each other again. That's one of the risks in my profession.'

The blood rushed from her face at his words, the anguishing memory of his crash in the Indy 500 came vividly back. She swayed toward him, reeling from the stabbing pain in her midriff.

His hands closed over the soft flesh of her upper arms and drew her the rest of the way toward him. Her head was tilted back to gaze into the handsome features while her hands spread themselves on the solid wall of his chest. For an instant they were like two statues, motionless in the beginning of an embrace.

Drawing her up on tiptoe, Mitch lowered his head to meet her halfway. A quivering magic raced through her when his mouth claimed her lips, persuasively warm and ardent. A longing filled Susan for the enchanted spell to continue, her breath completely stolen and her heart thudding against her ribs. Almost with reluctance, he released her lips.

His back was to the others and he spoke in a low soft voice that carried its message only to her ears. 'You aren't going to forget me. I won't let you.' In a louder voice, for the benefit of the rest of the family, he said, 'Goodbye, Susan.'

Then she was released and he was moving away. The flesh of her arms was cold where his hands had been and the coldness began to penetrate to the bone. Only her mouth still tingled with warmth.

Her gaze was riveted to him, mesmerized by the mystical power he held over her that made her respond physically to his touch.

I'm engaged. I'm going to marry Warren. The words were almost a chant, spoken silently toward off the bewitching effect Mitch had on her.

Susan marveled at the way he had dissociated himself from their kiss of a second ago. She was stunned by it and he was smiling cheerfully and bidding everyone a last goodbye as he slid behind the wheel of his sleek sports car.

When he reversed out of the drive, Mitch waved, but it was a wave that encompassed them all. Susan wasn't singled out for any last attention. She stood in the driveway with her family until he was out of sight, the hushed silence darkening the cloud of depression at her heels.

Susan was the first to turn away, hot tears in her eyes. 'I'll forget him,' she declared to herself. 'Maybe not tomorrow, but he's wrong. I'll forget him.'

It was a bold statement made in desperation. Her heart didn't believe a word of it, but her mind wouldn't listen to her heart. There were too many things it might have to admit if it did.

Yet when she arrived at the office that morning, Susan didn't say anything to Warren about Mitch leaving. She didn't think she would be able to listen to his caustic remarks about the Indy man. As often as she had tried, Susan couldn't despise Mitch as much as Warren did. Mitch had disrupted her life, but she couldn't bring herself to hate him for it.

10

S usan! Warren is here. Are you ready yet?' her mother called from the bottom of the stairs.

Rising from the edge of the bed where she had sat for the last ten minutes in huddled silence, Susan walked slowly to the hallway door and then hesitated.

'I'll—I'll be down in a minute,' she answered.

Why hadn't she phoned him and said she wasn't feeling well? she asked herself for the hundredth time, as she walked to the mirror above the chest of drawers. It wasn't that she was actually sick. She simply didn't feel like going out tonight.

To be truthful, Susan hadn't felt like going out Saturday night or Thursday night or Tuesday night or either of the weekend nights before that. This Sunday evening was proving to be no different. The second Sunday since Mitch had left.

'That has nothing to do with it,' Susan whispered angrily the instant she had the thought.

But she was beginning to believe that it had more to do with it than she wanted. Every room in the house was haunted by Mitch's ghost. She could hardly bear Warren's embraces any more. They left her feeling vaguely revolted and sick. Warren hadn't changed, so she must have.

With a sigh, because that there was no sense putting off going downstairs, Susan turned away from the mirror and walked dispiritedly into the hallway and down the steps. The living room was empty and she guessed that her mother had invited Warren to wait in the family room where the others were.

Following the lower hallway, Susan paused in the open archway of the family room, her troubled eyes going to the man sitting with military erectness next to her father. A second later Warren glanced up, saw her and smiled.

'You look lovely, Susan,' he said warmly, but she felt nothing.

'I hope I didn't keep you waiting too long,' she said quickly.

'I didn't mind in the least,' Warren replied, rising to his feet. 'I planned—'

'Sssh!' Greg interrupted loudly, gesturing with his hand for Warren to be quiet while he frowned in deep concentration at the transistor radio in his hand.

'What is it?' Her father leaned forward eagerly. 'The results at Pocono?' At Greg's nod, Simon said, 'Turn it up.'

'—Snyder's victory today was marred by a disastrous crash on the hundred and seventy-fifth lap that involved seven cars. The leading cars were lapping the slower traffic when Binghamton lost control of his car in the turn and bumped into Braden, sending him to the wall. That started a chain reaction——-'

'Oh, no!' Susan tried to muffle the cry with her hand, but it rang clearly in the hushed room. Warren stared at her stricken expression, a darkening cloud drawing blackly over his face. But she didn't see him.

'Turn it up!' cried Amy, reaching for the radio and bumping the station dial.

'Leave it alone!' Greg yelled, hurriedly turning the dial back to the station.

'—listed in critical condition. Now to the baseball scores,' the sportscaster said.

'Oh, Simon,' Beth Mabry glanced earnestly at her husband, 'you don't suppose it's Mitch? It couldn't be, could it?'

His gaze bounced away from hers as if unwilling to guess. 'Try another station, Greg,' her father urged.

Susan was rooted to the floor, frozen by the cold terror that held her motionless. If her heart was beating, she couldn't feel it, as she prayed that Mitch was all right.

Not even the shattering ring of the telephone in the living room could prod her into action. It was Amy who raced from the room, muttering that Cindy, her girl friend, had chosen a bad time to call. Warren touched Susan's arm.

'Are you ready?' he asked impatiently.

'Not now!' She looked at him blankly, stunned that he would want her to leave before she found out if Mitch was hurt. 'I can't leave now.'

'What——-' Warren began with biting arrogance.

But Amy's voice interrupted him. 'Susan, it's for you. It's long distance.'

Susan crossed her arms, running her hands shakily over her elbows. 'Who is it, Amy?' she called back.

'Someone named Mike O'Brian. Do you know him?' was the answer.

Her eyes widened in instant recognition of the man Mitch had identified as his pit boss at the hospital. She pivoted sharply around and raced to the living room alcove where Amy stood holding the telephone receiver in her hand.

Susan took it and quickly put it to her ear. 'Hello?'

'This is Mike O'Brian, Susan,' the vaguely familiar voice answered on the other end. 'I don't know if you remember me, but I work——-'

'Yes, yes I remember you,' she broke in nervously.

'I'm calling for Mitch.'

Susan interrupted again. 'Is he all right? We heard about the crash on the news a minute ago and—Is he all right?' she repeated desperately. Her fingers tightened on the receiver.

'Susan——-' the man hesitated. 'He's asking for you.'

Fear rose to strangle her throat. 'How badly is … is he hurt?'

Her question was met by another moment of silence. 'I think it would be best,' Mike O'Brian answered slowly, choosing his words with care, 'if you could come right away, that is if you can come.'

'Of course I'll come. I'll leave right away,' Susan rushed, choking back a frightened sob.

'I'll tell him.'

'Mike, wait! What hospital——-' But there was a click at the other end and the line went dead.

Slowly Susan replaced the receiver, turning to find the anxious faces of her family gathered around her. Behind them was Warren, a black mask stealing over his rugged features.

'Mitch? Is he——-' Greg began, and stopped.

'I—I don't know how badly he's hurt.' Susan shook her head absently, trying to elude the nausea that made her want to faint. Her frightened brown eyes sought out her father. 'Mike said he was asking for me and wants me to come as soon as I can. I told him I would. Daddy,' her voice broke for a second, 'I don't know which hospital.'

He was instantly at her side, a supporting arm curving around the back of her waist. 'Don't worry about it, honey. You'll be able to find that out when you get there. First let's get you there.'

'You don't actually intend to go to Pennsylvania, do you?' Warren accused.

For an instant, she could not honestly understand why he was objecting. Mitch needed her and her place was there. Then she realized what that meant.

'Yes, I am going,' she answered very calmly.

Her father, with his usual perception, sensed what was about to come and immediately began dispersing Susan's audience.

'Beth, go upstairs and pack Susan's things. Amy, give your mother a hand.' He tossed a set of car keys to Greg. 'Get my car out of the garage, Greg, and warm it up while I use the phone in the study to call the airlines and see how soon Susan can get a flight.'

During the flurry of orders, Warren continued to glare at Susan, angered that she would think of betraying him this way and arrogantly confident he could change her mind. Despite her fear for Mitch, Susan was feeling a crazy kind of peace. Nothing Warren could say or do would ever take it away from her.

'As your future husband, Susan, I'm asking you not to go,' he said crisply.

At his reference to their coming marriage, Susan glanced down at her tightly clasped hands, turning them slightly so she could see the rainbow sparkle of her engagement ring. She smiled faintly.

'I'm going.'

'You're my fiancée,' Warren reminded her tautly. 'I'm not going to stand by while you rush to another man's side.'

'I think you've missed the point.' Susan raised her head, serenely meeting the volcanic darkness of his eyes. 'I'm not asking you to stand by. I'm just wondering how I could have been so blind these past weeks.' She slipped the ring from her finger and held it out to him. 'I'm sorry, Warren, that we both had to find out this way.'

'You can't mean you're in love with this man!' he demanded incredulously, ignoring her outstretched hand.

'That's exactly what I mean.'

'But you're in love with me! You've told me that repeatedly. How can you suddenly say you're in love with someone else?' he accused angrily.

A gentle smile of understanding spread over Susan's mouth at Warren's outraged bewilderment. 'I was once warned that secretaries invariably become infatuated with their bosses, especially when they're men like you. I fell so heavily in love that I nearly missed the real thing.' It was so amazingly clear now that she marveled that she hadn't seen it before. A cold chill chased away the thought. 'I may be too late now.'

'I'm warning you, Susan, if I take that ring now, it's all over between us,' he stated icily. 'Don't expect to come running back to me if you discover that you're wrong.'

'I understand perfectly,' she nodded.

His mouth tightened into an ominous line. Then he reached out and snatched the ring from her fingers. Without another word he strode angrily toward the front door, slamming it loudly.

Her father appeared in the hallway arch, a bright twinkle in his eyes when he glanced at the front door. Turning to Susan, he winked broadly in approval and she couldn't help smiling back.

'There's a flight that will be leaving in fifty minutes,' Simon Mabry told her as he walked to the base of the stairs. 'Beth, do you have Susan's suitcase packed? We have to leave for the airport now if we want to catch the first flight.'

'I think so,' her mother called back, appearing seconds later at the top of the stairs with Amy right behind her. 'I do hope I haven't forgotten anything, Susan,' she said anxiously as she hurried down the steps carrying the overnight bag.

'We haven't time to go over it now,' her father decreed, taking the bag and motioning for Susan to follow him.

'Call us as soon as you can, Susan, and let us know how Mitch is,' her mother requested, hurrying out the front door behind them. 'And give him our love.'

'I will, Mom,' Susan promised.

The car was in the driveway, the motor running. Greg hopped from behind the wheel as Simon Mabry walked around the front of the car.

'Boy, was Warren mad when he left!' Greg declared in a slightly delighted tone. 'Did you ditch him, Susan?'

'Yes,' she said simply, opening the passenger door and sliding into the seat.

'Don't forget to phone!' Beth called to Susan as Simon Mabry put the car in gear.

Susan nodded that she would.

'And tell Mitch he can recuperate at our house again!' Greg added.

They reversed out of the drive and headed down the residential street. As they turned on to the highway, Mr. Mabry glanced at his watch.

'I think we'll make it in plenty of time,' he assured Susan with a quick smile.

During all the turmoil, there had not been one question or comment from any of her family. Susan shifted self-consciously in her seat.

'Dad,' she began hesitantly, 'I think I should explain.'

'You don't need to,' he interrupted her. 'I think I'd already guessed which way the wind was blowing.'

'But how?' she frowned.

'If there's one thing more obvious than a couple gazing into each other's eyes, it's two people avoiding each other. And,' he breathed in with a faint shrug, 'that goodbye kiss Mitch gave you practically clinched it for me. He's one future son in-law that I'm going to like.'

'Daddy,' chilling fear crept into her voice, 'he just has to be all right.'

'He will be.' It was almost a promise.

Everything had happened so fast that Susan hadn't been conscious of time. Now the interminable waiting had begun.

The jet plane might have had wings, but it couldn't travel fast enough for her. She alternated between cold dread that she was already too late, that Mitch might have died before she was able to tell him she loved him, and clinging hope that love wouldn't let him slip away. The very fact that Mike O'Brian had avoided telling her how badly Mitch was injured made her imagine the worst.

Tears of relief pricked her eyes when the plane taxied to a stop at the terminal building. She knew she couldn't afford to panic.

First she had to find a telephone and discover which hospital Mitch was in and, she hoped, find out his condition. Then she would need to take a cab. She forced all other thoughts from her mind. She had to take one step at a time, she told herself as she impatiently followed the disembarking passengers ahead of her.

The gate area was filled with other passengers waiting to board the plane. Susan hurried to the counter to ask the airline attendant for the location of the nearest telephone. The words never were uttered as a man separated himself from the other waiting passengers and walked to her side.

The golden brown head tilted itself to one side, a bright glow in the blue eyes that crinkled at the corners. 'Hello, Susan,' Mitch said softly.

For a long second, Susan stared at him in disbelief. 'Mitch?' And he smiled. She took a hesitant step toward him. 'Wh—what are you doing here?'

The light in his eyes danced wickedly. 'I've been meeting every incoming plane that you could have possibly caught from Indianapolis.'

She took another step closer, wildly searching for any sign of concealed injury, cuts, bruises, anything. 'But I thought you were hurt? Mike. ...'

'Mike never said I was hurt,' Mitch interrupted complacently. 'He only said I was asking for you.' His voice lowered to a husky caress. 'I've been asking for you for a long while. This time you finally heard me.'

'Do you mean this was all a trick?' Susan accused in astonishment. An anger began to build at all the unnecessary anguish she had gone through. 'You let me believe you were critically injured just to get me out here. I think that's cruel! It's—it's—'

'It's the mark of a desperate man,' Mitch answered quietly, reaching to take hold of the hand she was flinging wildly about. 'A man who's very much in love and who knows the woman he loves loves him, only he can't get her to admit it. And he's terrified she'll marry someone else. You do love me, don't you, Beautiful?'

'Yes!' she snapped.

'What about Warren?' He turned her left hand slightly and saw her bare wedding finger.

'He was there when Mike telephoned,' Susan answered curtly. 'I gave him back his ring.'

'He must have been furious.' The grooves around his mouth deepened, those engaging, dimpling lines appearing in the lean cheeks.

'He was,' she admitted. Under the charm of his smile, she began to feel her anger fade. 'Oh, Mitch, what about the accident at the race? The radio said a car bumped yours and sent it into the wall.'

'That's true,' he agreed, cupping her cheek in his hand. 'But I just kissed the wall and continued on with the race. The other collisions occurred behind me. I didn't win, but I finished the race.'

Her love couldn't be held in check any longer and Susan rushed into his inviting arms. He held her against him, burying his head in her hair.

'I was so terrified,' Susan murmured against his chest. 'I was afraid I'd never be able to tell you that I love you.'

'Tell me,' he ordered, raising his head and forcing hers up with a thumb under her chin.

With her head tilted way back, Susan gazed adoringly into his face. 'I love you, Mitchum Alexander Braden.'

The blue eyes smouldered. 'Now, repeat after me: Will you marry me?'

'Yes,' she laughed gaily.

A smile flashed across his face as he shook his head. 'You're supposed to propose to me. I told your father you would.'

'When?' she asked with a doubting smile.

'About twenty minutes ago when the airline confirmed you were on this plane. I didn't want your family worrying about me, so I called,' Mitch told her lazily. 'Now, are you really going to make a liar out of me to your father?'

'Will you marry me?' she asked dutifully.

'I thought you'd never ask,' Mitch chuckled.

Unmindful of the other passengers in the terminal, he claimed his kiss to seal the bargain. At the moment, nothing and no one else existed except each other.

About the Author

Janet Dailey, who passed away in 2013, was born Janet Haradon in 1944 in Storm Lake, Iowa. She attended secretarial school in Omaha, Nebraska, before meeting her husband, Bill. The two worked together in construction and land development until they "retired" to travel throughout the United States, inspiring Janet to write the Americana series of romances, setting a novel in every state of the Union. In 1974, Janet Dailey was the first American author to write for Harlequin. Her first novel was *No Quarter Asked*. She has gone on to write approximately ninety novels, twenty-one of which have appeared on the *New York Times* bestseller list. She won many awards and accolades for her work, appearing widely on radio and television. Today, there are over three hundred million Janet Dailey books in print in nineteen different languages, making her one of the most popular novelists in the world. For more information about Janet Dailey, visit www.janetdailey.com.

OPEN ROAD
INTEGRATED MEDIA

Open Road Integrated Media is a digital publisher and multimedia content company. Open Road creates connections between authors and their audiences by marketing its ebooks through a new proprietary online platform, which uses premium video content and social media.

Videos, Archival Documents, and New Releases

Sign up for the Open Road Media newsletter and get news delivered straight to your inbox.

Sign up now at
www.openroadmedia.com/newsletters